Death of a Trickster

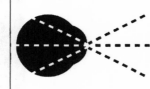

This Large Print Book carries the Seal of Approval of N.A.V.H.

Death of a Trickster

Kate Borden

WHEELER
PUBLISHING

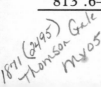
Copyright © 2004 by The Berkley Publishing Group.

Published in 2005 by arrangement with The Berkley Publishing Group, a division of Penguin Group (USA) Inc.

Wheeler Large Print Cozy Mystery.

The text of this Large Print edition is unabridged. Other aspects of the book may vary from the original edition.

Set in 16 pt. Plantin by Christina S. Huff.

Printed in the United States on permanent paper.

Library of Congress Cataloging-in-Publication Data

Borden, Kate.
    Death of a trickster / by Kate Borden.
      p. cm.
    ISBN 1-58724-958-8 (lg. print : sc : alk. paper)
    1. Women mayors — Fiction. 2. Teenage boys — Crimes against — Fiction. 3. Large type books. I. Title.
PS3602.O685D43 2005
    813′.6—dc22   2005000293

Remembering C.A.N.

As the Founder/CEO of NAVH, the only national health agency solely devoted to those who, although not totally blind, have an eye disease which could lead to serious visual impairment, I am pleased to recognize Thorndike Press* as one of the leading publishers in the large print field.

Founded in 1954 in San Francisco to prepare large print textbooks for partially seeing children, NAVH became the pioneer and standard setting agency in the preparation of large type.

Today, those publishers who meet our standards carry the prestigious "Seal of Approval" indicating high quality large print. We are delighted that Thorndike Press is one of the publishers whose titles meet these standards. We are also pleased to recognize the significant contribution Thorndike Press is making in this important and growing field.

Lorraine H. Marchi, L.H.D.
Founder/CEO
NAVH

* Thorndike Press encompasses the following imprints: Thorndike, Wheeler, Walker and Large Print Press.

Chapter 1

Indian summer wrapped itself around Cobb's Landing like a cozy fleece blanket. The sultry air softened the sky to stone-washed denim blue, a perfect backdrop for the russet, red, orange, and yellow autumn leaves that still covered the New England hillsides in crazy quilts of color.

The air hummed in a siren song, tantalizing the residents of Cobb's Landing with the promise of carefree summer fun. A day to shuck the nose-to-the-grindstone routines of fall as easily as the thick wool sweaters already taken out of mothballs to ward off previously chilly days and colder nights that foretold the coming of a long hard winter.

Mischief was brewing in the sultry air.

At ten o'clock on that late-October Thursday morning, teachers at the Cobb's Landing elementary school struggled to drum the three R's into the heads of students more intent on gazing out open windows than at the blackboard.

During a particularly mind-numbing session of sixth grade English, Nicky Turner glanced at the dark-haired girl sitting across from him, but she was engrossed in watching Nicky's best friend, Charlie Cooper, wiggle his ears.

Nicky tore a corner from a page in his notebook, rolled it between his fingers into a tight ball then slipped it into the plastic juice-box straw that lay in his fist. Faking a slight cough, Nicky raised his fist to his lips and turned toward Charlie seated two rows away. Nicky took careful aim. Charlie yelped and clutched his right ear as if he'd been stung by a vicious hornet. And immediately retaliated with his own well-aimed spitball. The class erupted in laughter. The dark-haired girl rewarded Nicky with a shy smile.

Carole Ann Cartwright — Mrs. Cartwright to her students — new to Cobb's Landing elementary but not to the pranks of restless eleven-year-old boys, turned away from the blackboard where she'd been diagramming "The quick red fox jumped over the lazy brown dog." to face her class. She clapped her hands once — a sound like the crack of a bullwhip — for attention.

"Nick Turner and Charles Cooper will

report to the principal's office immediately. The rest of the class will get ready for our nature walk to Alsop's woods to collect leaves and seeds for our botany scrapbook."

The two dozen sixth-grade students gleefully abandoned diagraming sentences, thumped their English books shut, and ran outside whooping and hollering. Nicky and Charlie sat glumly on straight-back chairs in the principal's outer office while phone calls were made to their mothers.

On Main Street, shop windows were being decorated for Halloween.

Peggy Jean Turner, mayor of Cobb's Landing and the owner of Tom's Tools and Hardware, nudged her black cat Pie off the checkout counter as the phone began to ring. Peggy called out to her lifelong friend and neighbor, Lavinia Cooper, who was drinking a cup of coffee.

"Lovey, I'm up to my elbows in pumpkin glop. Will you get the phone?"

Lavinia answered with a perfunctory "Tom's Tools." Pause. "No, this is Lavinia Cooper, Mrs. Turner is busy right now." She listened for a moment, then put her hand over the receiver and turned to Peggy.

"PJ, it's the school. Our boys are in the principal's office."

"What for?"

Lavinia repeated the question and listened to the response.

Pie took advantage of Peggy's distraction to leap back onto the checkout counter, worming her sleek body between the cash register and the beach ball–sized pumpkin Peggy was cleaning. A paw snaked across the newspaper covering the counter to snag an errant pumpkin seed. Peggy glared at the cat. Pie squeezed her eyes shut, feigning innocence and invisibility.

Lavinia hung up the phone. She turned to Peggy with a smile on her face. "Spitballs. Charlie and Nicky were pelting each other with spitballs during English class. They've been expelled for the day." She looked at her watch. "I've got to get to the hospital for my nursing shift. Can you pick up the boys? I'll hold Pie while you clean up. You've got pumpkin on your nose."

Peggy headed for the bathroom off the stockroom, the sweep of her long skirt sending dust motes swirling across the wooden floor like the sultry breeze skittering eddies of fallen leaves outside on the town square.

Lavinia handed over Pie into Peggy's clean hands.

"Lovey, what am I going to do with

those boys for the rest of the day? I can't lock them in the stockroom."

Lavinia plucked her car keys from her purse as she held open the door of Tom's Tools with her hip. "You're the mayor, you'll think of something appropriate. Community service? Whatever you decide, Chuck and I will back you a hundred per-cent."

As Peggy headed out the back door to her car parked behind the hardware store, a low-slung, black sports car pulled up in front of Ian's Booke Nooke across from Tom's Tools, the driver ignoring the NO PARKING DURING TOURIST SEASON signs fastened to every lamppost. A few minutes later, a couple walked arm-in-arm into Clemmie's Cafe. By the time Peggy returned with Nicky and Charlie, the car and driver were gone.

"I can't believe we're missing the field trip," Nicky grumbled.

"Yeah," said Charlie. "Just because Mrs. Cartwright is married to the new police chief, she doesn't have to be so mean. It was only a spitball."

Peggy looked at the boys. "Today's the day you were going to Alsop's woods, right?"

The boys nodded.

"You remember, Mom," said Nicky, "you signed my permission slip. We're supposed to be collecting leaves and seeds for our science project."

"My dad will have a major fit if I flunk science," said Charlie.

"Well, boys," said Peggy, "I'll tell you what I'm going to do. I'm going to help you both pass science. Nicky, go into the stockroom and get two rakes. Charlie, you take this box of leaf bags."

Peggy took one of the rakes from Nicky and handed it to Charlie. She put her arms around the boys' shoulders and walked them to the door of Tom's Tools. "You're going to spend the rest of the day on the town square raking and bagging leaves. I'm sure you'll find enough there for a dozen science projects."

Nicky looked at Charlie. They both knew better than to argue with Peggy.

"Don't forget to clean out the horse trough," said Peggy, smiling to herself as she watched the boys — heads down, muttering about the unfairness of it all — cross Main Street, dragging the rakes behind them, tines up, bumpity-bumping along the uneven sidewalk.

Peggy went back to cleaning her pumpkin. Pie, having escaped the stockroom when Nicky fetched the rakes, clawed her way onto the checkout counter to curl up, tail draped over the edge of the counter, for a nap. Peggy was soon up to her elbows — once again — in pumpkin glop.

"Exploiting the child labor market, are we?"

"Max! I hate it when you do that."

"Do what?" An innocent smile appeared on Max's elfin face. He stood in front of the checkout counter, nattily attired in a navy pinstripe suit, pale blue shirt with white collar and cuffs and sporting his trademark red silk bow tie. His close-cropped white hair was neatly brushed forward to a point on his forehead.

"Pop up out of nowhere. How do you do that? I didn't hear you enter the store."

"One of my lesser, but many, talents, Mayor." The smile broadened.

"What's on your mind, Max?"

"It'll keep. Why aren't those boys in school? Is it a holiday?"

Peggy chose to sidestep Max's inquisition, although she was tempted to retort that idle hands were the devil's tools. "Speaking of holidays, Max, I have a favor to ask of you."

"Do you need to borrow money?"

"*Max.* Not everything revolves around money."

"It does in my business." Max had taken over the Citizen's Bank in Cobb's Landing earlier in the year.

"How goes it at the bank, Max?"

"These low interest rates are killing me." Max clutched his chest dramatically. "In the past few months we've refinanced almost every mortgage in Cobb's Landing. I'm practically giving money away." Max moaned softly for added effect.

Peggy gestured with her elbow toward a plastic pumpkin on the far end of the checkout counter. "Have some candy corn, Max. My treat. You'll feel better."

"Don't mind if I do." Max helped himself to one of the trick-or-treat-sized cellophane packets. "It's my favorite. How did you know?"

"Lucky guess." Peggy remembered the exact moment Max had mentioned his fondness for candy corn, but it was her turn to play innocent. "About that favor. We, that is, the town council, would like you to be a judge at the pumpkin float on Halloween night."

"Pumpkin float? Are you talking about one of those hideous creations made of chicken wire, pastel Kleenex flowers, and yards of sagging crepe paper?" The very idea made Max grimace.

Peggy shook her head. "No, Max. Not that kind of float. I forget you haven't been in Cobb's Landing an entire year. The pumpkin float is just what it sounds like. We float Halloween pumpkins on the Rock River. The ones that go the fastest and farthest win prizes." She baited the hook with something she knew would get Max's undivided attention. "The pumpkin float is a big tourist attraction."

Max brightened at the mention of tourist revenue. "I'll promote it on the Colonial Village Web site."

It had been Max's idea to turn Cobb's Landing — founded in 1757 by Josiah Cobb, a button maker from England — into Colonial Village, a themed tourist attraction with residents dressed in colonial-inspired costumes, as a way to save the town from impending economic death. Max had converted the defunct and derelict button factory — a two-story red brick structure on the bank of the Rock River, once powered solely by its wooden waterwheel — into a thriving hotel. Colonial Village had its problems — enforced covering of satellite dishes and the inconvenience of no cars on Main Street during tourist hours was a giant pain — but thanks to Max, the hard work of the town residents, and the new reproduction furniture factory, Cobb's Landing was slowly getting back on its feet.

"Do pumpkins really float?" asked Max.

"You could look it up on the Internet," said Peggy.

"Sarcasm does not become you, Mayor." Max helped himself to a handful of candy corn. "I would be honored to serve as a judge for the pumpkin float. What other festivities have you planned for Halloween?"

"There's the after-school costume contest on the town square, trick or treating on Main Street, and tours of the haunted house, followed by the pumpkin float on the Rock River, then everyone goes to the Halloween dance in the school gym."

"We could have fireworks after the pumpkin float," said Max.

Peggy shook her head. "I don't think that's a smart idea, Max. You remember what happened the last time we had fireworks in Cobb's Landing."

Max raised his hands in surrender. "You have to admit, Mayor, that evening ended with a real bang." Max glanced at his watch. "I have an appointment at the bank.

16

We'll talk again tomorrow." With a wink and a wave, Max was gone.

Peggy took a break and walked up Main Street to Alsop's Bakery to get lunch for the boys. As she approached the open front door, Peggy could smell the mouth-watering aroma of freshly baked sugar cookies. The display windows flanking the bakery's center entrance were decorated for Halloween. On the left was an aerial view of Cobb's Landing at night, tiny houses in orderly rows on either side of Main Street, over which hung a giant cookie witch riding a broomstick; the window on the right featured a haunted house made of gingerbread.

Inside the bakery, Gina Alsop was spreading orange frosting on chocolate-vanilla-swirl cupcakes.

"Gina, your windows look great," said Peggy. "I haven't even finished carving my first pumpkin."

"I'll tell Maria. She'll be so pleased. The gingerbread house was her idea. It gives us something to do together while Lew's gone."

"Have you heard from him lately?"

"He calls when he can. The Middle East is so far away. But I keep in touch with the other wives in his National Guard unit.

That helps. I never knew how hard it is to be a single parent. I don't know how you do it, Peggy."

Peggy smiled. "You do what you have to. When is Lew due back?"

"He should be home by Christmas at the latest. I try not to count the days."

Peggy looked at the daily specials listed on a chalkboard. "What's good today?"

"You're too early for pizza, I haven't turned on the ovens yet," said Gina. "How about a couple of roast beef and provolone sandwiches on focaccia? It's something new I'm trying out for the leaf peepers. A change from the usual ham and swiss on rye. I baked the bread fresh this morning."

"Make that three, Gina, I haven't had lunch either. And six of your Halloween sugar cookies. They smell so good!"

"Three sandwiches? I thought these were for you and Ian."

"No, they're for Nicky and Charlie."

"Aren't they on the field trip?"

Peggy told Gina the whole story.

"Spitballs?" Gina laughed. "Kids. I'm sure Maria will tell me all about it when she gets home from school." She wrapped the sandwiches and put them in a bag with the cookies. "Peggy, have you got a minute?"

Peggy nodded.

18

Before Gina could say any more, Maria burst into the bakery, eyes wide, her breath ragged.

"Mama," Maria gasped, "we found a body in the woods!"

Chapter 2

Peggy and Gina stood in a clearing in Alsop's woods, Maria between them clutching her mother's hand, gazing at the body lying in a nest of age-stained, rusty orange, maple leaves.

"Well, I never," said Gina. "In all the years Papa Luigi has owned these woods . . ." Gina swallowed hard. "Well, I never." Her voice faltered. She squeezed Maria's hand, bending to plant a kiss on her daughter's glossy dark hair. "Maria, let's join your classmates."

Gina and Maria headed toward the group a few yards away. The girls were huddled together; one was crying, her sobs slowly subsiding into erratic hiccups. The boys were running around the woods, edging as close to the body as they dared before they were summoned by a short blast from Mrs. Cartwright's whistle.

Peggy knelt at the edge of the leaf pile to get a better look. The body — she couldn't tell at first glance if it was male or female — was lying face down, covered by a long, flowing black cape with a high starched collar. Both black-gloved hands were extended over its masked head, appearing as if the body had been trying to crawl out of the leaves.

Peggy shivered despite the sweat-inducing warmth of the Indian summer afternoon sun. She shook herself to recover her composure — I'll be damned if I'm going to faint *this* time, she thought, remembering her involuntary reaction to seeing the body on the waterwheel a few months earlier — and looked at the body again.

Something — actually, several somethings — didn't seem quite right.

Peggy sniffed. Aside from a faint hint of eau de sun-heated polyester mingled with the dry, dusty scent of crushed dead leaves, there was no odor. Although Peggy's up-close-and-personal experience with dead bodies was limited to finding her late husband, the Tom of Tom's Tools, dead in their kitchen after his electrifying experience with a souped-up waffle iron — and that, having happened almost ten years earlier, was becoming a dim memory — and the body on the waterwheel the previous spring, she knew one thing: Dead bodies *do* smell. To put it bluntly: They stink.

Another thing. The girth of the body didn't match the height. After all her years in the hardware store, Peggy was good at eyeballing measurements, and these didn't add up. The body appeared to be of average height for an adult male, but looked like a poster child for Slim-Fast.

A slender broken branch fell from the maple tree above, landing with a hollow thunk on the body.

Peggy leaned forward to pick up the branch.

A hand grabbed her upper arm. "Don't touch that, Mrs. Turner. You're interfering with a crime scene."

Peggy flinched. She looked up to see Mrs. Cartwright leaning over her.

"You should know better," Mrs. Cartwright said in her well-practiced "I can send you to the principal's office" tone of voice. "Chief Cartwright is on his way. He'll be very upset if you've destroyed any evidence."

Although Peggy was not about to get into a public tiff with Nicky's teacher, she wasn't easily intimidated. "Take your hand off my arm," Peggy said, staring pointedly at the grasping fingers, "I haven't touched anything."

Mrs. Cartwright reluctantly complied with Peggy's request, but continued to track Peggy's movements, her fingers flexed to grab Peggy's arm if she dared to defy her.

Peggy rose and brushed the dirt from the front of her long skirt, feeling faintly ridiculous in her colonial costume when Mrs. Cartwright was dressed in sensible slacks. Everything about Carole Ann Cartwright was sensible. Sensible slacks, sensible shoes, sensible shirt, sensible waterproof watch on her wrist, her whistle suspended from a woven lanyard that looked like it had won a merit badge as a scout craft project. She looks like the type who drinks only decaf and eats prunes every morning, thought Peggy.

When she heard the approaching police car siren, Mrs. Cartwright raised the whistle to her lips.

Peggy put her hands over ears, stifling an impulse to pull the lanyard tight, cutting off Mrs. Cartwright's air supply.

Henry Cartwright, the new chief of police in Cobb's Landing, jumped out of the police car tooting his own whistle.

My God, it's like two raptors calling

each other, thought Peggy, what is this? *Jurassic Park*? She noted that the Cartwrights sported matching lanyards.

Henry Cartwright greeted his wife with a brisk pat on her shoulder. "The medical examiner is on his way. I hope no one's contaminated the crime scene." His last remark was directed at Peggy.

"I caught Mrs. Turner trying to touch the body," said Carole Ann, "but I was able to stop her in time."

"Very good," said Henry with a quick nod of approval. Carole Ann beamed. "Let's see what we have here," he added. Henry looked down at the knife-edged crease in his uniform trousers and the spit-polish shine on his shoes. Then he looked at the leaf pile. His practical side won out. "I think we'll wait for the medical examiner."

"I don't think that's necessary," said Peggy. She quickly hitched up her skirt and knelt in the leaves. Without waiting for permission from anyone, she picked up the forked maple branch that had fallen on the body. Using the branch like a lever, she slipped it under the body and rolled it over.

Underneath the black cape, the body was clad in a black turtleneck and black leggings. Shoeless, its feet were covered with bright red socks.

Peggy pulled the Count Dracula mask away from the victim's face.

Everyone gasped.

Staring back was an eyeless skull. A very clean skull.

Peggy looked up at Henry Cartwright. "I think you'd better call off the medical examiner. His coming here will be a waste of everyone's time."

Peggy pushed up the right leg of the black leggings. Etched into the thigh bone were the words "Property of CLHS."

The initial chorus of gasps from the students slowly modulated into giggles and guffaws. Peggy rocked back on her heels, laughing until her stomach hurt and tears streamed down her face. The Cartwrights remained stone-faced and unamused.

"Th-th-th-that's B-b-b-buddy!" Peggy said, her speech punctuated by a fresh wave of giggles.

"Who is Buddy?" said Henry.

Peggy wiped the tears from her face with the back of her hand. "Buddy is the high school science department mascot. He's a skeleton that's been around since . . . I was in school here. This is nothing more than a Halloween prank." Peggy gathered Buddy in her arms. "I'll see that Buddy gets back to school in time for science class tomorrow."

Henry Cartwright's face was as red as Buddy's socks as he stalked to his police cruiser to ward off the impending arrival of the medical examiner. Henry hated being made a fool of, especially by a woman. He'd get to the bottom of this prank pretty damned quick, and he'd show that mayor who was boss in Cobb's Landing. Henry nodded emphatically as he picked up his handset.

Chapter 3

With Buddy safely back in the science classroom at the high school, Peggy headed for
the town square to check on Nicky and
Charlie.

They had an impromptu picnic on the
leaf-free grass.

Nicky peeled the top layer of bread off
his sandwich. "What's this stuff inside,
Mom?"

"It's meat and cheese, Nicky. Eat it."
Peggy handed each of the boys a bottle of
lukewarm lemonade. "When you finish
your sandwich, I've got Halloween
cookies."

" 'Le Dèjeuner sur l'Herbe.' Manet would
have loved painting this little group."

Peggy looked up to see Ian standing a
few feet away with an amused expression
on his face. Peggy felt her face flush, even
though she'd been seeing Ian off and on
for a few months and they were somewhat
of an item in Cobb's Landing.

"Lunch on the grass. One of Manet's

most famous works." Ian dropped down on the grass next to Peggy. "I always thought the men's faces looked like the Smith Brothers on the cough-drop box."

"Manet? Is he the one who painted water lilies?"

"That's Monet. They were contemporaries, and everyone gets them confused."

Peggy offered Ian a cookie. The boys grabbed their Halloween cookies and went back to bagging leaves. "It's such a beautiful day. How about a cookout tonight?"

"Ah, Peggy, about tonight," said Ian. "Something's come up. A last-minute business meeting."

"Oh?" Peggy licked the orange frosting off her cookie. The frosting was the best part. When she was a little girl, she always begged to lick the bowl. Caramel frosting was her favorite.

"I'm sorry, Peggy."

"Another time." Peggy shrugged, balled the sandwich wrappers, and put them in the bag.

"I've got to go. I'll call you later. Thanks for the cookie." Ian kissed Peggy on the cheek before heading up Main Street to the Booke Nooke a block away.

As Peggy walked back to Tom's Tools,

she saw a black sports car idling at the curb outside the Booke Nooke. Ian locked the door of his store, got in the car, and the driver took off. Some business meeting, thought Peggy, her good mood souring.

Peggy reopened her own store, determined to enjoy what was left of the day. She looked for Pie, but couldn't find her anywhere. Peggy decided to go home and finish carving her pumpkin outside in her backyard. She hefted the pumpkin and felt the weight shift. A small dark head, capped in pumpkin glop, popped out. Oh Pie, let's get you home for a bath.

Peggy was giving Pie a quick bath in the kitchen sink when Lavinia came in through Peggy's back door.

"PJ, haven't you finished carving that pumpkin? You were starting it when I last saw you hours ago."

"Lovey, it's been one of those days. Must be something in the air."

"Chuck's going to fire up the grill tonight. Could be the last cookout of the season. Have you got any onions?"

"Look in the vegetable bin in the fridge."

"Dry the cat and come over. You can tell me all about your day while I make hamburger patties."

Peggy wrapped a wriggling Pie in an old

towel and briskly rubbed her dry. Pie stretched to rub noses with Peggy before scampering into the backyard to roll in the crackly leaves littering the browning grass. Peggy chuckled softly and hung up the towel to dry, then went upstairs to change clothes.

Through the open windows in her bedroom, Peggy heard the sounds of fall — or was it summer? — riding on the sultry air that held the faintest scent of burning leaves. Had it been a spring in her childhood, Peggy would have grabbed a piece of chalk to make a hopscotch on the sidewalk where she and Lavinia would have played until dinner. They'd lived next door to each other all their lives and shared the same memories. Peggy heard the whomp of a baseball hitting a glove as Nicky and Charlie played catch, her golden retriever Buster yapping while he ran between the boys hoping to catch the ball, the crackle of leaves when Pie leapt into them. Peggy hated the thought of being closed behind storm windows for winter, but if she left the screens up her heating bills would require a second mortgage she could ill afford. She took a deep breath of the heavenly fresh air, exhaled in a sigh of pure contentment, then headed for the gate in the backyard fence that separated her yard from Lavinia's.

"Life is short, eat dessert first." Lavinia reached into her freezer and handed Peggy a cherry Popsicle. "Found the last two of these in the back of my freezer this morning when I got out the ground beef to thaw. C'mon, it's too nice to stay inside. Next week we'll probably be huddled in front of a fireplace drinking hot cocoa." Lavinia grabbed her Popsicle and a piece of chalk, heading for her front door with Peggy on her heels.

They played hopscotch until Chuck came home to start the fire in the grill.

"I hear Buddy went AWOL today," Chuck said while he arranged the pile of charcoal in the brick barbeque pit he'd built himself.

"Buddy? Who's Buddy?" asked Lavinia.

"You remember, Lovey. The skeleton in the high school science class," said Peggy.

"It's been a long time since high school."

"Not that long, honey," said Chuck, winking at his wife.

"What happened to Buddy?" asked Lavinia.

"Peggy knows, she was there," replied Chuck.

"Start at the beginning," said Lavinia, "don't leave anything out."

"I went to Alsop's to pick up some sand-wiches for Nicky and Charlie."

"I thought they had a field trip today," said Chuck.

"Later, honey," said Lavinia, "go on, PJ."

"While I was talking to Gina . . . Lovey, do you have enough for two more? I've got extra ground beef in my freezer."

"Sure. Who do you want to invite?"

"Gina and Maria. With Lew away, Gina seems lonely. I thought she could use a night out."

"Great idea. Go call her. Use the kitchen phone," said Lavinia.

"Is Maria coming here for dinner?" asked Nicky.

"I'm going to call her mother now," re-plied Peggy.

Nicky dropped his baseball glove and ran through the gate into his house.

Peggy tracked Nicky's flight with a small shrug and went into the Cooper's kitchen. While she was on the phone, Charlie ran inside and upstairs to his room.

Peggy went back outside a couple of minutes later. "Gina said thanks and asked for a raincheck. She has to take dinner to Papa Luigi."

"She could have brought him along," said Lavinia.

"I suggested it. She said he wasn't feeling well. Nothing serious, a summer cold or something like that."

"Papa Luigi must be in his late seventies by now," said Lavinia. "But he still lives in his house in the woods. He always was an independent sort. I'll make a note to have one of the visiting nurses check on him. With old people there's always a danger of pneumonia."

"While the boys are inside," said Chuck, "I want to know what happened with the field trip."

"Charlie and Nicky were expelled today for shooting spitballs in English class," said Lavinia. "PJ, you tell the rest of it while I get us cold beers."

"Spitballs?" said Chuck, a smile tugging at his lips. "When I was Charlie's age, we all had pea shooters."

"I put the boys to work raking leaves on the town square," said Peggy. "It was good exercise, and they collected enough samples for their botany scrapbooks."

"Good thinking, Peggy. Thanks."

Lavinia came outside with three bottles of cold beer. "Now I want to hear about Buddy."

Charlie poked his head out the kitchen door. Peggy noticed he'd changed his shirt. "Mom? What have you got for us to drink?"

"There's lemonade in the refrigerator. Bring some for Nicky, too."

"We had lemonade for lunch."

"All right, Charlie. You can have a Coke. But just one. And, bring one for Nicky."

"What time is Maria coming?" asked Nicky.

Peggy looked at her son. Comb tracks showed in his freshly washed hair, and he was wearing a clean shirt. "I'm sorry, honey, Maria's not coming. Another time, sweetie."

Charlie came out with three Cokes in his hands. "I brought one for Maria."

Lavinia and Peggy exchanged a quick glance. "Charlie, Maria can't make it tonight. Put the extra Coke back in the fridge. You and Nicky can split it with your burgers. Why don't you two play ball until dinner's on the table."

"Coals will be ready in ten minutes," said Chuck.

"I made macaroni salad, and I've got chips," said Peggy. "I'll go get them."

When everyone was settled at the Cooper's picnic table munching hamburgers,

Lavinia said, "PJ, now I want to hear about Buddy."

"Who's Buddy?" said Charlie and Nicky in unison.

Peggy told the Coopers and Nicky about finding Buddy in the leaf pile in Alsop's woods.

"He was dressed in a Halloween costume?" said Lavinia.

"A long black cape, black leggings, and a black turtleneck. With a Count Dracula mask over his face. And red socks on his feet. I think it was someone's idea of a Halloween joke."

"Geez, I miss all the exciting stuff," said Nicky.

"Today was your own fault, Nicky," said Peggy. "We'll talk about it later." She looked around the table. "What do you say we walk to the general store for ice cream? My treat."

"I want to ride my bike," said Nicky.

"Me, too," said Charlie.

"Watch out for cars," said Lavinia.

"We'll meet you at the general store," said Peggy.

Peggy, Lavinia, and Chuck set out at a leisurely pace, turning left onto Acorn Lane when they reached the end of their block on Maple Street. A block later, they headed right on Main Street. As they walked toward the general store, the auto-timed streetlights began to glow, then brightened to full strength.

"I am going to hate it when daylight saving time ends this weekend," said Lavinia.

"You say that every year," said Chuck, putting his arm around his wife.

"I mean it every time, Chuck. I know, I grew up in Cobb's Landing — we all did — but I hate living like a mole in the winter. It's dark when I get up, dark when I leave the hospital."

Chuck planted a kiss on his wife's cheek. "Enjoy the evening, honey. We could have frost on the ground by morning."

"Gather ye rosebuds, right?" Lavinia gently prodded Chuck with her elbow.

"Whatever that means," said Chuck.

Most of the businesses on Main Street were locked for the night, including Clemmie's Cafe, but lights were still blazing in the general store and Alsop's Bakery.

"Nicky and Charlie were here," said the clerk to Peggy, "they got ice cream and left. Nicky said you would pay for it."

Peggy nodded and ordered a double-dip waffle cone topped with sprinkles. One scoop of pumpkin, one vanilla.

36

"Same for me," said Lavinia.

"A double chocolate for me," said Chuck.

They walked down Main Street toward the Rock River, licking their cones, stopping to look at the Halloween decorations in the shop windows.

Peggy turned to Chuck. "How's the haunted house coming?"

"We'll get it finished this weekend," said Chuck. "It's going to be scarier than last year. Bob at the gas station is going to dress like that Freddy guy in the movies." Chuck was the head of the volunteer fire department, and the haunted house was one of their annual fund-raisers.

When they reached the former button factory, now Max's bed-and-breakfast hotel, they walked down the path to the river.

"Water looks low this year," said Chuck.

"I hope that won't mess up the pumpkin float," said Peggy.

Chuck grinned. "Nah. Just means I'll have to change my strategy."

"What strategy?" asked Peggy.

"That's for me to know and you to find out," said Chuck. "You're not walking away with the adult pumpkin prize this year, Peggy Jean, you've got competition."

They were crossing Main Street when a

motorcycle roared toward them. The driver swerved at the last minute, missing Lavinia by inches.

"Honey, are you all right?"

"I'm fine, Chuck. Really. Who was that?"

"Peggy, you've got to do something about that kid."

"What kid?"

"Roger Cartwright, the new police chief's son. He thinks he's a Hell's Angel. The high school principal has banned that bike from the school grounds."

"I'll talk to Henry Cartwright tomorrow," said Peggy with a sigh. There were times when being the mayor of a small town really sucked, and this was one of them.

Heading for home, they reached the turn onto Acorn Lane as a black sports car traveled slowly down Main Street.

"That's the second time today I've seen that car," said Peggy.

"Didn't you know?" said Lavinia. "It belongs to Missy. She's back in Cobb's Landing. Max transferred her here from Providence."

Peggy's heart fell to her shoes.

Chapter 4

Indian summer vanished as suddenly as it appeared. Chuck's prediction of frost proved accurate the next morning. Peggy shivered as she closed her bedroom windows and thought of the salacious ditty that began "when the frost is on the pumpkin." She'd get those screens off and the storm windows put on this very weekend. Winter was on its way.

But Indian summer left behind its calling card. The air of mischief lingered in Cobb's Landing.

Buddy had taken up residence in the horse trough on the town square.

Peggy first heard about it when the phone rang at seven.

Nicky yelled from the kitchen. "Mom, it's for you."

"Be right there." Peggy was halfway down the stairs. It was easier to answer the phone in the kitchen rather than turn around and go back to her bedroom. She whispered to Nicky "who is it?" as he handed her the receiver.

"Old Mrs. McIntyre." Nicky made a face and went back to pouring Cheerios in a bowl.

Gazing heavenward for strength, Peggy listened as Mrs. McIntyre shrieked into her ear. Finally Peggy was able to say, "Yes, Mrs. McIntyre. I'll look into it right away. You have a nice day." Peggy stuck out her tongue at the receiver before hanging up the phone.

"What's the matter, Mom?"

"Mrs. McIntyre is a royal pain. And don't you ever quote me, or I'll cut off your allowance."

Nicky grinned.

"She says there's a body in the horse trough. C'mon, Nicky. Let's go check it out."

Nicky's eyes lit up. "All right!"

"Put on your jacket, it's cold this morning."

"Why didn't Mrs. McIntyre call the police?"

"She doesn't like the new police chief. She wants her son back in that job."

"I miss him, Mom. When is Mac . . ." Nicky caught the look on Peggy's face. "I mean Mr. McIntyre, coming back?"

"I don't know, Nicky. I don't think anyone knows." Peggy reached for her jacket

40

and keys. "Let's take the car. I'll drive you to school this morning. I packed your lunch last night and put it in the refrigerator. Don't forget it."

Peggy parked on Main Street, ignoring the posted regulations. It was too early for tourists to be up and about. Only old Mrs. McIntyre was on the prowl at dawn, ostensibly walking her yappy, little, ankle-biting mongrel dog Poopsie, but in reality the dog walking was an excuse for Mrs. McIntyre to snoop on her neighbors.

The lights were just coming on in Clemmie's Cafe. Peggy needed coffee. Badly. But first she had a body to check out.

Buddy was reclining in the horse trough. One hand behind his head, the other — to put it succinctly — resting on his crotch. Nicky snickered, Peggy shook her head and sighed. How much more of this would she have to put up with before Halloween?

Once again, Buddy was dressed as Count Dracula.

Peggy pulled up the legging to look for the etching on the thigh bone. It was Buddy all right. She handed Nicky the car keys. "Open the trunk, Nicky." She locked Buddy in the trunk of her car, his head

41

resting on a bulging shopping bag. "How about breakfast at Clemmie's this morning?"

"You mean it, Mom? Can I have waffles?"

"You may have anything you like. But you need to promise me one thing."

"What's that, Mom?"

"Look me in the eye, Nicky." Peggy put her hands on Nicky's shoulders and gazed into his big brown eyes. "I want you to solemnly promise no more spitballs or acting up in school."

Nicky knew Peggy wasn't kidding around. "I promise."

"If you're expelled again you'll be grounded for a month. No television, no computers, no playing with Charlie. Is that clear?"

Nicky nodded.

Peggy hugged her son. "C'mon. Let's get breakfast."

Clemmie's Cafe was a Cobb's Landing institution. Like the general store, it had been around as long as anyone could remember. But unlike the general store, Clemmie's had closed when the button factory shut down. People always have to eat, but people out of work do not eat out. Clemmie's Cafe had reopened, under new

42

management, the previous spring as part of Colonial Village. The red-and-white checked curtains in the front windows were new, but inside it was the same old Clemmie's everyone remembered. Formica counter with wood swivel seats on the left, wooden booths for four or six lining the right wall, tables for two along the front next to the windows. The menu was standard stick-to-your-ribs American/New England fare. Nothing fancy, nothing nouvelle. Chicken with dumplings, meatloaf and mashed potatoes, choice of vegetables, and pie or cobbler for dessert. Apple and cranberry in the fall and winter, rhubarb in the spring, assorted berries in the summer. You could depend on Clemmie's.

Nicky wanted to sit in a booth. He faced the street, while Peggy had her back to the front door.

Nicky ordered waffles with a side of sausages. The pitcher of maple syrup was already on the table. Peggy inhaled her first cup of coffee, then held out the empty cup for a refill. She decided to treat herself to something she'd never take the time to prepare at home, a western omelet.

The front door opened, sending a gust of chilly air across the cafe. Nicky looked up from his nearly empty plate, put down his fork, and waved. "Mom, there's Ian." Nicky's smile faded. Peggy turned to look. Ian wasn't alone. Missy was right behind him. Peggy picked up a piece of whole wheat toast and began buttering it with swift strokes.

Ian spoke first. "Good morning, Peggy. Hi, Nicky."

Nicky concentrated on drinking his milk.

"Peggy, you remember Missy."

Peggy's mouth was full of buttered toast.

Missy nodded in Peggy's direction, her loose black curls brushing her shoulders, then put her hand on Ian's sleeve. "I'm absolutely famished. Let's get a table. I do hope they make decent Eggs Benedict here."

Ian escorted Missy to a nearby table, looking over his shoulder to mouth at Peggy, "I'll call you later."

Peggy put out some money to cover her bill and said to Nicky, "Let's go, you'll be late for school."

After dropping Nicky at Cobb's Landing elementary, Peggy headed for the high school. Before going inside, she quickly stripped the costume from Buddy and left it in the truck of her car.

In the science room, only the teacher was present, busy grading papers.

"Milt, I've brought Buddy back again."

Milt Flask put down his red pencil. "Where was he this time?"

"In the horse trough."

Peggy hung Buddy on his stand, then perched on the edge of Milt's desk. "We've got a problem. I need your help." Peggy and Milt talked quietly for a few minutes, then Peggy went home to change into her colonial costume for another day at Tom's Tools.

Chapter 5

Henry Cartwright was standing at parade rest outside Tom's Tools when Peggy arrived to open up. In her left arm Peggy cradled the still-uncarved pumpkin, her right hand was curled around the handle of Pie's carrier.

"Forgive me if I don't shake hands," Peggy said. "Would you take the pumpkin so I can unlock the door?"

Henry handled the pumpkin as gingerly as a bomb, avoiding any contact with his starched and perfectly pressed uniform.

"Thanks. You can put the pumpkin on the checkout counter."

Henry complied, looking for something to wipe his hands.

Peggy handed him a paper towel. "What can I do for you this morning?"

"We need to get something straight, Mayor Turner."

"What's that, Henry?"

"I am the police chief in Cobb's Landing."

"Of course you are," Peggy said as she

46

opened Pie's carrier. Pie sprang forth to rub against Henry Cartwright's trouser leg. Henry stiffened and glared at the cat, his foot twitched as if he were harboring thoughts of drop-kicking Pie across the room. Peggy grabbed Pie and stroked her soft black fur. "As you were saying, Henry."

"You had no business going to the horse trough this morning without calling me first."

"Henry, it was the same prank as yesterday. Someone dressed Buddy in a Halloween costume and put him in the horse trough. There was no foul play involved. If there had been, I would have called you immediately."

Henry refused to be appeased.

"Finding Buddy was not a police matter," said Peggy. "But, I'll tell you what is."

Henry listened.

"There's a security problem at the high school. Milton Flask, the science teacher, swears his classroom was locked yesterday afternoon when he left for the day. If that's true, then how did someone get into the high school and into the classroom to kidnap Buddy?"

"I'll investigate, Mayor. But you need to keep your nose out of police business."

"We both work for the town, Henry. The only difference is you get paid. Let me know what you find out."

Henry Cartwright turned on his heel and walked out of Tom's Tools, letting the screen door bang shut behind him. A gust of chilly air swept through the hardware store. A further reminder that summer was gone.

Peggy went to the stockroom looking for the storm door. She found it next to the Christmas decorations and hauled it outside. In a few minutes she had it hung and the screen door tucked away until spring. She washed the grime off her hands and went back to carving her pumpkin.

"I think this is where I came in yesterday."

Peggy started at the sound. "Max, I'm going to tie a bell around your neck."

Max grinned and reached for a packet of candy corn. Peggy tapped the back of his hand with the wooden spoon she was using to clean the pumpkin. "First we talk, then you get a treat. I've got a bone to pick with you."

"*Moi?* What have I done?" Max adored playing the innocent.

"It's what you haven't done," said Peggy.

Max looked confused.

48

Gotcha, thought Peggy, delighted that for once she had the upper hand in dealing with Max. "Why didn't you tell me that Missy was back?"

"Is that what's bothering you?" Max brushed Peggy's concern aside with an airy wave of his hand. "Purely a business matter. A temporary assignment. She'll be gone before you know it. It's nothing for you to get ruffled about." Max helped himself to candy corn.

Peggy cocked her head and looked at Max. "Hold still, Max." She picked up a grease pencil and made a few marks on the pumpkin, then covered it with a sheet of newspaper.

"I want to see what you're doing."

"Come back this afternoon, Max. It'll be finished then."

When Max was gone, Peggy went to work. An hour later she stood back and looked a her handiwork. Then she went to her car and returned with the bulging shopping bag.

By noon the Tom's Tools store window was decorated for Halloween. It featured Count Dracula sitting on a tombstone, posed like Rodin's *The Thinker*. But instead of using a mask for the face, Peggy had carved the pumpkin head to look exactly like Max in one of his impish moments.

She picked up a second pumpkin and quickly cleaned it. This one would be for the pumpkin float. Working from memory, Peggy soon had a Halloween-inspired caricature of Missy's face adorning the pumpkin. She took a flashlight and put it inside — for the actual pumpkin float she'd use a lit candle — then stood back to get the full effect. She chuckled to herself at the thought of Missy's head bobbing down the Rock River.

Chapter 6

"Gina, I feel like an idiot. I really meant to pay you yesterday for the sandwiches and cookies." Peggy handed Gina a twenty-dollar bill. "Will this cover it? And don't forget the two bottles of lemonade."

"Thanks, Peggy. I wish I could say it's on the house, but with Lew away . . ." Gina reached into the bakery case for two Halloween cookies which she wrapped and put in a bag. "Give these to Nicky for an after-school snack."

"Nicky will love them." Peggy paused. She really didn't know Gina all that well and hesitated to pry into her personal life. "Gina, are you making out all right? Is there anything I can do?"

"Lew and I haven't been apart for more than a day or two since we were married. It gets hard at times, especially since he's so far away. I try not to watch the war news on television, but I can't help myself. Then I worry more. You were very nice to invite us over for burgers last night. I know

51

Maria would have enjoyed it."

"How about another time? Tonight if you're free. I've got chicken and rice cooking in my crock pot. There's more than enough for four."

"Peggy, we can't tonight. It's Friday, pizza night, one of our busiest nights. I need Maria here to help me with the orders."

Peggy changed the subject. "How is Papa Luigi feeling?"

"He says it's only a cold and I fuss over him too much."

"Lovey said she'd have one of the visiting nurses look in on him. Just to make sure his cold isn't turning into anything more serious."

"I'd be grateful," said Gina, "although Papa Luigi might feel differently. You know how independent he is. I swear he's getting worse as he gets older. He's so secretive about everything. I tried to clean house for him the other morning, his desk was a mass of paper, and he practically threw me out. Said he was perfectly capable of taking care of his own affairs." Gina sighed. "He dotes on Maria. She goes there every afternoon and takes his supper to him. I've asked him to stay with us while Lew's away, but he wouldn't hear

52

of it. Said he couldn't leave his house in the woods."

Several customers entered the bakery.

Peggy picked up the bag of cookies. "My door is always open, Gina. If you want some time to yourself, send Maria over. Nicky would be glad to see her."

The chilly, gray weather had brought the leaf peepers out of the woods and into Cobb's Landing. Max's horse-drawn buggies were carting tourists up and down Main Street at five bucks a head. Peggy pulled her shawl closer to her shoulders — the wind had a definite bite to it — and hurried back to her store. It was time for hot apple cider.

While the cider was warming, Peggy lettered a sign and hung it on her storm door: HOT SPICED APPLE CIDER — $2.00. By mid-afternoon she'd refilled her urn three times.

"Oh, that smells good," said Lavinia as she entered Tom's Tools, briskly rubbing her hands to warm them. "It's nippy today. Is my credit good for a cup of cider?"

"Help yourself, Lovey. On the house. How was your day?"

"Busy. Suddenly everyone wants a flu shot. Why they bother, I don't know. The shots only protect against last year's strain. Who knows what those nasty little microbes will mutate into this year." She sipped her cider. "I see you finally got your window done." Lavinia giggled. "Has Max seen it yet? It's a perfect likeness."

Peggy grinned. "I was feeling devilish."

"Where did you get the costume?"

"From Buddy. It's what he was dressed in yesterday in Alsop's woods. I've got another one just like it in the trunk of my car."

"The red socks are a nice touch," said Lavinia, heading for more hot cider. Then she did a double take. "You've got another costume?"

"You don't know what happened this morning. Buddy was found in the horse trough, dressed again as Count Dracula. Old Mrs. McIntyre called at seven to demand that I do something about it."

"Oh, geez," said Lavinia. "Talk about a rotten way to start your day. That woman is — and always has been — a busybody." Lavinia began to smile. "PJ, are you thinking what I'm thinking? It's almost Halloween, right?"

"Right."

"Well?"

Peggy and Lavinia looked at each other for a long moment, grins on their faces, then the two women high-fived each other.

"When shall we do it?" asked Lavinia.

"How about next Friday night?" said Peggy. "After the pumpkin float. While everyone's on the way to the dance at the school gym. Will Chuck help us?"

"Let's leave Chuck out of it. We'll do it ourselves, just like we did before."

"You're on, Lovey."

"Have I got this straight? Buddy has been kidnapped twice in two days?"

"I wouldn't have believed it, Lovey, if I hadn't seen it for myself. And returned him to the science room both times. I talked to Milt Flask this morning. He says he locked his classroom before he left yesterday."

"And this morning Buddy was in the horse trough?"

"You got it, Lovey."

"Which means someone got into the high school last night."

"That's exactly what I told Henry Cartwright this morning. He was waiting here in a snit when I came to open up."

"What was he in a snit about?"

"Telling me he was the police chief and I should have called him about finding Buddy in the horse trough. He was really telling me to mind my own business and stay out of police matters."

"Of all the nerve. Did you remind him who signs his paychecks?"

"Not exactly. I did point out that we both worked for the town, but he was the one who got paid."

"Sounds like Henry has a problem with women in authority," said Lavinia. "But we've got more serious problems brewing in Cobb's Landing."

"Like what?"

"I'm not exactly sure."

"Lovey, stop beating around the bush. Out with it."

"I stopped to see Papa Luigi this afternoon on my way home from the hospital."

"How is he?"

"He's got a bad cold. I told him to get lots of rest and drink plenty of fluids. If he felt worse, to come to the hospital and we'd take care of him. He got a little testy."

"That's what Gina said."

"When did you talk to her?"

"About noon today. I went to the bakery to pay her for the lunch I bought yesterday for the boys."

"PJ, my head's a sieve these days. I'll pay for lunch. You did enough picking up the boys at school and putting them to work for the afternoon."

"Tell you what. You can spring for pizza this weekend."

"Deal. Extra-large super-supreme with everything but anchovies?"

Peggy nodded.

"Let's get back to Papa Luigi," said Lavinia. "What did Gina say?"

"She asked Papa Luigi to stay with her and Maria while Lew was away, but he refused. He didn't want to leave his house," said Peggy. "Gina went over there to tidy up, and he practically threw her out. But she said he dotes on Maria and Maria goes there every day to take him some food."

"That's true, PJ. Maria arrived while I was there. She looked so cute in a bright red sweater with a hood, carrying a basket with a hot meal Gina had prepared."

"So? What the problem?"

"Maria was afraid of something. I think we should tell Gina."

"Oh, Lovey. That's all Gina needs right now. I get the feeling she's burying herself in the bakery because she's terrified of what may happen to Lew, and she's clinging to Maria for strength and support. I don't think Gina can cope with anything else."

"You may be right, PJ. But I'm concerned about Maria."

"Why?"

"Maria asked me to give her a ride from Papa Luigi's. She didn't want to walk home by herself. She said there was a wolf in the woods."

"A wolf? Come on, Lovey. That's a fairy tale."

"To us it's a fairy tale, but to Maria it's real. She was afraid of something. Or someone."

Peggy went to the phone and dialed.

"Who are you calling?" asked Lavinia.

Peggy held up her hand to quiet Lavinia. "Hi Gina, it's Peggy. I'm taking Nicky to the mall tomorrow afternoon to pick out his Halloween costume. I know how busy you are, why doesn't Maria come with us?" Peggy listened to Gina's reply. "It's no trouble at all. Tell Maria I'll pick her up at your house at one-thirty. She'll have supper with us before I bring her home." With a satisfied look on her face, Peggy hung up the phone.

"I'm coming with you tomorrow," said Lavinia. "This is one mystery you're not going to solve by yourself."

Chapter 7

Peggy arrived at Tom's Tools before eight o'clock Saturday morning. Peggy tried to work only a half day on Saturday in order to spend time with Nicky, but there were times — when her budget was tight and she had bills to pay — that she stayed open all day. Today she'd close at one sharp to take everyone to the mall.

She put her key in the lock to open the front door and noticed a small brown envelope hanging from the doorknob. After she turned on the interior lights and flipped the door sign from CLOSED to OPEN, she stood at the checkout counter looking at the envelope. It felt sort of squishy, like there was something soft inside. Should she have it tested first? Dunk it in a pail of water? Wear gloves when opening it? Get a grip, she muttered to herself, this is Cobb's Landing. She tore into the envelope. Inside was a folded note, penned in red ink: "Here's the finishing touch for your window." The note was signed in a florid scrawl that — if you squinted and looked at it sort of sideways — might be interpreted as "Max."

Nestled in the note was a red silk bow tie.

Peggy howled with laughter and put the tie around the Count's neck. It took three tries before she got the bow just right. No clip-ons for Max. She added candy corn to her shopping list, then filled the urn with apple cider.

Business was brisk on that last Saturday in October. People were reminding each other to set their clocks back an hour before they went to sleep. "Are you sure we set them back?" "It's spring ahead, fall back. Right, Peggy?" It seemed as if all of Cobb's Landing was determined to hang their storm windows that weekend. "*Farmer's Almanac* says we're in for an early and long winter this year."

Chuck and some of the volunteer firemen, including Bob from the gas station, came in for materials for the haunted house. "Say, Peggy," said Bob, "you'd better think about getting your snow tires put on pretty soon. I've been counting the rings on the woolly bears. Gonna be a hard winter."

Chuck interrupted Bob's windup to a

sales pitch. "C'mon, Bob, you can sell Peggy a new set of snows another time. We've got work to do." Chuck turned to Peggy. "Thanks for getting the kids out of our hair this afternoon. We want the haunted house to be a surprise. It's going to be better than ever. When we're finished there, we'll get your storms put up."

Peggy opened her mouth to say thank you.

"Don't mention it, Peggy. We're glad to help." Chuck corralled his crew and they headed for the haunted house.

Peggy glanced across the street at Ian's Booke Nooke several times that morning, but with all the leaf peepers milling up and down Main Street, she never caught sight of Ian.

Promptly at one, she unplugged and washed out the apple cider urn and closed up shop for the weekend. She hurried home to change clothes. One more week and she'd be free of her colonial costume until spring. One more week and she could park on Main Street again. But as much as they groused over the minor inconveniences, the town residents had to admit that Max's vision of Colonial Village had saved Cobb's Landing. Five months earlier, Peggy would have thought twice before taking Nicky to the mall. It was hard to be a parent who always said no, we can't afford it. Peggy still clipped coupons and watched her pennies and bought "on special" whenever she could, but now her budget had a little wiggle room and she could afford the luxury of closing the hardware store early for an afternoon of fun.

Nicky waited impatiently for Peggy to get home. His hair was neatly combed, his jeans were clean, and he was wearing his good sweatshirt instead of his favorite with paint spattered on the front and holes in the elbows. "Hurry, Mom, we're going to be late. You promised Maria you'd pick her up at one-thirty." Peggy smiled to herself as she bounded up the stairs two at a time. Nicky was growing up, and unless she was mistaken, puppy love was in the air.

She quickly changed into jeans, sweatshirt, and sneakers. When she went into the kitchen, Lavinia and Charlie were already there. "New jeans, Charlie? You look nice."

They arrived at Maria's house promptly at one-thirty. Maria was wearing the red, hooded sweater Lavinia had described. It contrasted nicely with Maria's dark hair.

Peggy drove with Lavinia in the front passenger seat. Maria sat in the back, between Nicky and Charlie. At the start of the thirty-minute trip to the mall, the boys were uncommonly silent. Lavinia broke the ice by asking Maria what she was going to wear for Halloween.

"Mama was going to make me a costume, but she's too busy at the bakery. Papa Luigi said he would pay for one. Last year I was a ballerina."

"Last year I went as the Tin Man from *The Wizard of Oz*," said Nicky. "Mom made my costume with stuff from the hardware store. It was pretty cool."

"I went as Tom Sawyer," said Charlie. "I felt like a dork."

"You looked adorable, and you won a prize, Charlie," said Lavinia. "Maybe this year you three could be a team. What do you think?"

They spent the rest of the trip discussing it.

The mall was packed. Peggy finally found a parking space. As malls go, this one was no great shakes, but it was the only one in the sparsely populated New England county. And it did have a food court and a movie theater with three screens.

The racks of Halloween costumes were the most popular spot in the chain discount store, especially since all costumes were marked fifty-percent off. Peggy and Lavinia began trying on outrageous Elvira/Morticia inspired fright wigs while the kids looked through the costumes.

Peggy went over to help Maria. "Have you seen anything you like?"

Maria held up a white costume, trimmed in gold.

"Princess Leia," said Peggy. "Try it on, Maria. It looks perfect for you. Nicky, Charlie! Come here, I've got an idea."

Veteran shoppers Peggy and Lavinia pawed through the racks. By the time they finished, the *Star Wars* trio — Princess Leia, Han Solo, and Luke Skywalker — was ready for Halloween.

"Mom, do we have to hang around here any longer?" said Nicky. "We want to go look at stuff."

"It's three o'clock. We'll meet you at the food court in an hour." Peggy whispered to Nicky, "Keep an eye on Maria, okay?" Nicky nodded, pleased with his assignment.

"Lovey, what are we going to wear this year?"

"Let's get wild," said Lavinia, holding up a slinky, black, Morticia Addams number. "I'm going to try this one."

Peggy looked through the racks again. Then she approached a harried clerk. "I'm looking for a Count Dracula costume."

"We had three, but they're all gone. I think one guy bought 'em all earlier this week. Good luck."

Lavinia came back with her costume bought and paid for. "I even got the wig, false eyelashes, and fake fingernails," she said. "Do you think I can convince Chuck to be Gomez?"

"Over his dead body," Peggy laughed.

"What are you wearing?"

"I can't decide. I'll think about it while I'm grocery shopping. You want to come with me?"

"I shopped yesterday morning. I'll see you in the food court."

Peggy went to the other end of the mall to do her grocery shopping. She wheeled her loaded cart to the car and opened the trunk. I could have sworn I locked this, she muttered to herself. She looked inside. The Count Dracula costume she'd taken off Buddy before returning him from the horse trough was gone. The first costume — from Alsop's woods — was now on display in her store window. She examined the trunk lock closely. There was no sign of a break-in. I must have forgotten to lock it, she thought. Peggy hated the idea of a sneak thief in Cobb's Landing, but with all the tourists about she would have to be more careful. She unloaded her groceries, locked her car, and headed for the food court.

Lavinia jumped up from a table as Peggy approached. Her expression was grim. "Maria is missing."

Chapter 8

"What do you mean, missing?" asked Peggy.

"I mean, no one knows where she is," snapped Lavinia. "Do I have to spell it out for you?"

"I told Nicky to keep an eye on Maria."

"Well, he didn't, did he?" Lavinia scanned the food court while she talked. "I sent the boys out to look for her. I told Nicky to start at the discount store and Charlie to go to the grocery. They're supposed to look in every store and report back here in half an hour."

Peggy headed for the food-court exit.

"Where are you going?" asked Lavinia.

"There are places the boys won't think of looking," Peggy replied. "You stay here, I'll be back in a flash."

Peggy went to the discount store and headed for the clothing department fitting rooms. She looked under every door for Maria's feet. Then she went to the ladies' room. No sign of Maria.

Peggy backtracked along the mall toward

the food court, stopping only long enough to run in and out of every store. Before she reached the food court, she saw an arrowed sign labeled restrooms pointing to the end of a short corridor lined with pay phones. Peggy ran into the room marked women. The small room was silent. Two of the stall doors were open, the third was shut. Peggy looked for feet and saw none. "Maria," Peggy called softly, "are you in here?"

There was silence. Then a faint response. "Mrs. Turner? Is that you?"

"Yes, Maria. It's me. Are you all right?"

Silence.

"Maria, are you sick?"

"Nooo."

"Can you open the door?"

"Is there anyone else in here?"

"No. We're all alone. Open the door, Maria."

The stall door slowly opened, and Maria poked her head around the door. When she was satisfied that Peggy was the only other person present, she came out of the stall.

Peggy looked at Maria's face. She dampened a paper towel and wiped the tears from Maria's pale cheeks.

"Tell me what happened."

"I was having such a good time, Mrs. Turner. Charlie and Nicky wanted to play a video game in the arcade. I said I'd meet them in the food court and went into another store. I was going to buy mama a present." Maria's voice faltered.

"Then what happened? It's okay, Maria. You can tell me."

Maria bit her lower lip. In a whisper she replied, "I saw the wolf."

"The same wolf from Papa Luigi's woods? Mrs. Cooper told me about it."

Maria nodded. "I ran out of the store, but he followed me and made me give him all my money. When he went away, I ran in here and hid."

"Who is the wolf, Maria? It is someone you know?"

"I can't tell you. He said if I told anyone something bad would happen."

"Maria, you've got to tell me who it is. I'm the mayor. I can do something about it. Is it someone in Cobb's Landing?"

Maria refused to say another word.

Peggy dried Maria's face and took her hand. "Come with me, we'll buy a present for your mother. What did you want to get her?"

When they arrived back in the food court, Charlie and Nicky were sitting with

Lavinia. They were all relieved to see Maria with Peggy.

"Maria was shopping for Gina and lost all track of time. Here she is, safe and sound." Peggy forced a smile. "I'm hungry. What shall we get to eat?"

Chapter 9

To Peggy, the drive back to Cobb's Landing seemed to take forever. In the backseat the kids were chattering away about Halloween; Nicky and Charlie were vying to escort Maria through the haunted house. Lavinia settled it by saying "why don't you all go together?"

It was almost seven when Peggy dropped Maria off at the bakery. Maria waved good-bye and quickly ran inside.

When they got home, Nicky and Charlie went up to Charlie's room to play computer games while Chuck watched football on television, the remains of microwave fried chicken on a plate beside him. Peggy and Lavinia sat in the kitchen.

"Want some chicken, PJ?"

"And French fries. I've got some in my freezer. I'll fix them at home and be right back."

Peggy went through the gate to her own backyard, clutching the bags from their shopping. She looked up and saw the lights reflected in the storm windows on her house. It was good to have caring neighbors.

Peggy fed Pie and Buster and put away her groceries while she fixed a big basket of fries.

After everyone had eaten, Nicky and Charlie went back to their computer game. Peggy, Lavinia, and Chuck sat talking in the Cooper's kitchen.

"I always thought it would be nice to have a daughter," said Lavinia. "But this afternoon I realized that daughters really are different than sons. PJ, I was a bitch in the food court, and I apologize. I really lost it when I thought something had happened to Maria. She seems so fragile and defenseless. Perhaps she's been overprotected by Lew and Gina."

"You can't blame them," said Chuck. "Maria is their only child."

"Charlie and Nicky are also only children," said Lavinia. "If the situation had been reversed and it had been Charlie who was late, I would have been angry but not as concerned. I guess I think that Charlie can take care of himself. Nicky, too."

Peggy nodded. "We raise boys to be tougher and more independent. But we have to remember they're only eleven. They also need to be protected."

"Are we going to tell Gina what happened at the mall this afternoon?" asked Lavinia.

"Absolutely not," said Peggy. "Like I said yesterday, Gina has enough on her plate right now. She may be over-protective of Maria, but she also depends on her. It's a complicated situation."

"I think you're wrong, PJ," said Chuck. "Maria's not your child. Gina has a right to know what's going on with her daughter. If Lew were here, I would be calling him right now."

"But that's just it, Chuck," said Peggy, "Lew isn't here. Do you want to be the one to tell Gina?"

Chuck was silent.

"There's something else to consider," said Peggy. "What if Maria is making the whole thing up? This wolf fixation could be a figment of her imagination or a bid for attention."

"I don't think that's true, PJ. Maria is a bright girl, she's an A student. When I saw her at Papa Luigi's yesterday afternoon, she was genuinely frightened."

"You're probably right, Lovey. Maria was upset this afternoon. I was just trying

73

to consider every angle. We've never had anything like this in Cobb's Landing. Until Colonial Village opened, we were a sleepy little town where everyone knew everyone else."

"And everyone knew everyone else's business," said Chuck with a grin. "PJ, I hear you had a call from old Mrs. McIntyre yesterday morning. We should make her the town crier."

They all laughed at the notion of old Mrs. McIntyre dressed as the town crier, standing on the square trumpeting the news every hour.

"What are we going to do, PJ?" asked Lavinia.

"Lovey, we're going to unmask a wolf," said Peggy. She turned to Chuck. "Have you heard anything at school?"

Chuck was the high school shop teacher.

"No, but I'll ask around," said Chuck. "No one messes with our kids and gets away with it."

Chapter 10

Sunday afternoon, while Nicky and Charlie were off playing with their friends, Chuck gave Lavinia and Peggy a sneak peak of the haunted house.

The haunted house was located between Alsop's woods and the old cemetery on the far side of town. It ended up on the Cobb's Landing delinquent tax roll after the button factory shut down and the prior owners were unable to find a buyer. Rather than face eviction, the owners skipped town one night giving rise to the rumors that the house was haunted. When the house was put on the auction block for unpaid property taxes, there were no bidders, and the house became town property.

The simple Cape Cod house had been repainted dove gray with black shutters during the Cobb's Landing spruce-up before the opening of Colonial Village. Chuck pulled the key from his pocket. "Bob's going to be at the front door taking tickets — we kept the price at a dollar for kids and two dollars for adults — in his Freddy costume. Max agreed to haul tourists back and forth from the town square in his horse-drawn buggies."

They went inside. It was spooky dark. The outside shutters were closed, and black cloth had been hung inside over all the windows. Chuck flipped the power switch. Eerie green light filled the rooms, and sounds of moaning were heard. Hidden fans set fake cobwebs and Spanish moss fluttering in the doorways. It looked like Disneyland's Haunted Mansion had been crossed with Madame Tussaud's.

A stout rope was threaded through stanchions to guide the visitors from one room to another and eventually out the back door. Fluorescent arrows were taped to door frames and walls to keep visitors moving in the right direction.

Peggy giggled. "This reminds me of a really bad old joke that ends with 'you've just been screwed by grandma.' "

Chuck groaned. "I haven't heard that one since high school. Peggy, you've got to get some new material."

As they walked through the house, Chuck gave them a verbal tour. "We'll have the witch and cauldron in the living room, Frankenstein in the dining room, ghosts in the parlor. And a few other surprises. The kids will love it." They ended up in the small backyard. "Out here we'll have hot cider and caramel apples for sale."

"You've outdone yourself this year," said Peggy. Lavinia agreed.

Chuck stayed behind at the haunted house to work on some finishing touches. Peggy and Lavinia decided to detour through Alsop's woods on their walk home.

The day was chilly and overcast. The wind was stripping the trees of their now-brown leaves, the glorious colors of fall having vanished as suddenly as Indian summer. The dead leaves crackled under the women's feet as they shuffled through the woods.

Peggy spied some acorns on the ground and put them in her pocket.

Lavinia smiled. "Remember when we used to make tea sets for our dolls out of hollowed out acorns?"

"What I remember is you mixing the acorn pulp with water and trying to get me to drink it. You said it was Indian tea. I knew better."

Lavinia spied a pile of leaves in the distance. She took off at a sprint and jumped into the pile. "Do it, PJ. I double-dare you."

Peggy jumped into the leaf pile and

rolled in it, just to hear the leaves crackle. Then she picked up a handful of leaves and threw it at Lavinia. An impromptu leaf fight ensued. When they'd had enough, they brushed the fragments of leaves from their clothing and continued on their walk.

As they approached the clearing where Papa Luigi's house was located, Lavinia put her hand on Peggy's sleeve and motioned to her to be quiet. She pointed at the house.

There, parked in the gravel drive in front of the house, was a black sports car.

Lavinia pulled Peggy behind a large maple tree.

"That's Missy's car," whispered Lavinia.

Peggy nodded.

The two women huddled behind the tree and waited.

In a few minutes Missy came through Papa Luigi's front door and stood on the porch. They heard her say, "I'll come by tomorrow morning with the final papers for you to sign. Then we can arrange the payoff."

Papa Luigi closed and bolted his front door. Missy got into her car and drove away.

Peggy and Lavinia stayed put behind the tree.

"What should we do?" Lavinia whispered. "I was hoping to look in on Papa Luigi to find out how he's feeling."

"Not a good idea," whispered Peggy. "Let's make like trees and leave the way we came."

They crept back through the woods until they were a safe distance away from Papa Luigi's house.

"What do you suppose that was all about?" asked Lavinia.

"I don't know," said Peggy. "But, if Missy's involved, you can be sure it's bad news for someone. And it's not going to be Papa Luigi. I'm going to get to the bottom of this."

"PJ, I'm chilled to my bones. Let's go to your house. I want to try on my Halloween costume while everyone's away."

Lavinia put on the dress and wig. "What do you think?"

"You look mah-vel-ous. You'll be the queen of the Halloween hop," said Peggy. "But that dress is pretty stark. You need something to jazz it up. Hold on." Peggy went upstairs to her bedroom. Ten minutes later she came back downstairs empty-handed.

"That was much ado about nothing," said Lavinia.

Peggy sat down on the couch, a puzzled expression on her face.

"What's up, PJ?"

"I've been robbed."

"What?"

Peggy sat shaking her head, unable to take it all in. "I went upstairs to get my charm bracelet for you. I thought it would add sparkle to your costume. But it's gone."

Lavinia sat beside her friend. "Are you sure?"

"Of course I'm sure. I've kept it wrapped in tissue in the same place in my jewelry box since we were in high school. Tom gave me that bracelet and all the charms on it." Tears slid down Peggy's cheeks. "Losing that bracelet is like losing the last part of Tom and all the happy times we shared. I haven't worn it since he died." Peggy began to sob.

Lavinia held her friend until the tears subsided. "Go blow your nose, PJ, then we'll talk." Lavinia went into Peggy's kitchen and plugged in the coffee pot.

Peggy sat with her hands wrapped around the hot coffee mug.

"Is anything else missing?" asked Lavinia.

"Not from the house. At least not that I can tell. But who knows? You live in a house all your life, you get used to things being in a certain place. Or you imagine they're still there. Sometimes when I look in my closet, I expect to find Tom's clothes hanging next to mine. Or see his dirty socks on the floor."

Nicky came in the back door. "Hi, Mom. Can I have a soda? I'm going over to play computer games with Charlie."

"Sure, honey. Take a soda for Charlie, too." Peggy paused while Nicky got the sodas out of the refrigerator. She wanted his full attention. "Sweetie, put those sodas down for a minute. I need to ask you something."

"What?"

"Have you seen my charm bracelet?"

"What's a charm bracelet?"

"Never mind, Nicky. Go have fun with Charlie."

Nicky bounded out the back door, through the gate, and into the Cooper's kitchen.

"PJ, you don't suspect your own son, do you?"

"Of course not. I just thought he might have seen it."

"I think you should call Henry Cartwright. This is a police matter."

Peggy shook her head. She wasn't up to

another session with Henry. Henry made her head hurt.

"What else is missing, PJ? You said before, 'not from the house.'"

"This is really weird. I had a Count Dracula costume in the trunk of my car. It's the one I took off Buddy when he was found in the horse trough. Yesterday at the mall, I went to put the groceries in the trunk and the costume was gone. I could have sworn I'd locked the trunk Friday morning."

Lavinia reached over to pat Peggy's hand. "Don't worry, PJ, it's not serious. It's called senility."

Peggy laughed.

"That's better," said Lavinia. "Now. What are you wearing for Halloween?"

"I haven't decided yet."

"Get in gear, PJ, you've only got five days left to make up your mind."

Chapter 11

The day before Halloween, Peggy had just unlocked the front door of Tom's Tools when the phone began to ring. She put Pie's carrier on the counter with one hand, grabbing the phone with the other.

"Tom's Tools."

"Good morning, Mayor."

"Max! Isn't this a bit early for a social call?"

"I'm sorry to trouble you, mayor, but I need you here at the hotel immediately." Without saying goodbye, Max hung up in Peggy's ear.

Peggy relocked her store and hurried down Main Street to Max's hotel.

The clerk on duty at the first-floor reception desk pointed to the second floor. "Max is upstairs."

Peggy hitched up the long skirt of her colonial costume, taking the stairs two at a time. The river side of the second floor was a cozy dining area, with tall windows overlooking the Rock River and the waterwheel, which had once supplied power for the button factory.

Max was standing at an open window next to the waterwheel. A teenaged boy, with a sullen expression on his face, sat at an adjacent table.

There was a body stretched out, face down, on the waterwheel.

Not again, thought Peggy, remembering the events of the previous spring. She stepped closer to look, steeling herself not to faint.

The long, black cape and the red socks were a dead giveaway.

Buddy was now lying on the stilled waterwheel.

"Max, call Henry Cartwright. This is a matter for the police."

The boy's expression changed from sullen to fearful. "Don't call my father."

"Who *are* you?" asked Peggy.

"Roger Cartwright," the boy mumbled.

"Max, I'll call Henry. This is out of my hands, and I'm not taking any responsibility for this mess."

The boy rose from the table, poised to run. Max pointed a finger, and the boy quickly sat down. Was it Peggy's imagination, or was there a faint whiff of ozone in the air?

Peggy went down to reception and called Henry Cartwright. Then she went back upstairs, one step at a time. "Henry will be here in a minute."

Even as she spoke, she heard the police siren approaching.

Henry Cartwright — starched, spit-shined, and neatly pressed — marched up the stairs.

Max ushered everyone into his office, away from the openly staring hotel guests ignoring their breakfasts. From the outset it was clearly Max's meeting. "I caught this young man red-handed on my property placing that mannequin on my waterwheel."

Peggy knew this was not the time to inform Max that the mannequin was in fact a human skeleton named Buddy, purchased from a medical supply house. She stood with her back to the wall and kept her mouth shut.

Max continued. "This is private property and that young man was trespassing. I am pressing charges. What do you intend to do about it?"

Henry was caught between a rock and a hard place. Peggy watched him squirm.

Duty won. Henry reached for his handcuffs.

"I don't think that's quite necessary," said Ian, entering the room.

"Who are you?" asked Henry.

"I'm Max's legal advisor," said Ian.

"I thought you ran the bookstore with the artsy name," said Henry.

"As a hobby, in my spare time," replied Ian. "Now, may I have a word with my client?"

Max and Ian left the room.

Henry glared at his son.

Roger studied the pattern in Max's Oriental carpet.

Peggy remained with her back to the wall and her mouth clamped shut.

Max and Ian returned. Max looked like he'd been sucking on a sourball. Ian placed a file folder on Max's desk and took over the meeting.

"My client feels, given the boy's age, that he be remanded to the custody of his parents. However, should there be any further misdeeds on the part of the boy and/or disturbances on my client's property, my client reserves the right to press full charges at a later date." Ian looked at Henry and Roger. "Are we in agreement?"

Henry put the handcuffs back on his belt. He clamped his hand around his son's upper arm and pulled Roger out of the chair.

"One moment," said Ian. "There is an agreement to be signed first." Ian opened the folder and handed a single sheet of paper to Henry. Max supplied the pen. Henry and Roger signed. In red. "Max, you and Peggy can be witnesses. I'll notarize the agreement."

Peggy and Max signed on the witness lines, Ian pulled out his notary seal and the deal was done.

Henry marched Roger down the steps and out of the hotel to the waiting police car. Since his arrival on the scene, Henry had not said one word to his son.

Chapter 12

Max ordered breakfast for three to be served in his office. "I do hope you like Eggs Benedict, Mayor. My chef makes a superb hollandaise sauce."

The mention of Eggs Benedict curdled Peggy's stomach, but she kept a smile on her face. She would not give Ian — or Max — the satisfaction of knowing she was jealous of Missy.

"Thank you for coming so promptly this morning, Mayor," said Max. "I know you must be very busy getting ready for the Halloween festivities. My hotel is booked solid through the weekend."

"Max, I want to thank you for the finishing touch for my store window."

"What are you talking about? I've been away for a few days on business. Did you finally finish carving that pumpkin you were working on last week?"

"Max, are you pulling my leg?" One look at Max's face told Peggy that Max was — for once — innocent. "You didn't send me one of your red silk ties?"

"*Moi?* I may be generous to a fault, but I do not share my haberdashery."

"My mistake," said Peggy. It was time to change the subject. "I restocked the candy corn at Tom's Tools. Do stop by. Max, would you mind if I took my breakfast to go? I really have a lot to do this morning, and I want to get Buddy back to the high school."

"I will deliver your breakfast personally," said Max.

As Peggy was leaving the hotel with Buddy zipped inside a black garment bag, Ian caught up with her.

"Dinner tonight?"

Peggy knew in her head that she really should say no, but her heart dictated otherwise. She missed Ian's company.

"Six o'clock all right? Don't you do anything except set the table. I'll provide dinner. I've missed you, Peggy." Ian leaned forward and kissed Peggy softly on the forehead. "See you at six."

For the third time, Peggy took Buddy back to the high school science classroom. "Milt, I thought you said you were keeping this room locked. What happened?"

"Peggy, I swear to you, I did lock it." Milt Flask pulled his key ring from his

89

pocket and held up a brass key. "Here's the key. There are only two. I keep the other one at home."

"Are you sure it's still there?"

"Positive. I have a ring of spare keys on a hook in my kitchen. It was there this morning when I left for school. Thanks for bringing Buddy back."

Peggy smiled. "Try to keep Buddy locked up until after Halloween, will you?"

As she was hurrying down the locker-lined school corridor, Peggy ran into Chuck.

"What brings you here?"

"Buddy got loose again, but he's back safely," said Peggy. "I'll tell you about it later." She waved and ran to her car.

She unlocked the hardware store door for the second time that morning. Again, the phone started ring.

"Tom's Tools."

"Peggy, it's Gina. Papa Luigi is missing."

Chapter 13

Peggy's head began to throb. "Gina, calm down and tell me all about it." Gina was crying too hard to speak. "Where are you?" Peggy listened. "I'll be right there." Peggy locked the door of Tom's Tools and ran up Main Street toward the bakery.

Gina stood at the bakery counter wringing her hands in the starched white apron she wore over her Colonial Village costume.

"Tell me everything, Gina."

"I went over to Papa Luigi's house this morning to take him some breakfast. I do that every morning. Maria takes him a hot meal after school for his dinner."

"And?"

"When I arrived, I knocked on the door but he didn't answer. I knocked again, then used my key and went inside. His bed was made and there was no sign of him."

"Maybe he went to run some errands?"

"His car was still in the garage."

"Maybe he went for a walk. It's a beautiful day."

"I left a note on his front door, telling him to call me. That was two hours ago, and I haven't heard a word. I keep calling his house every five minutes."

"Have you called the police?"

"There was no answer there, either."

"I'll get Henry. We'll be right back."

Peggy walked across the street to the building that served as the Cobb's Landing police station and also housed the town council offices. Henry was nowhere to be seen. Peggy left a note on his desk where he couldn't miss it, then picked up the handset that connected to the police cruiser.

"Henry Cartwright. Are you there?"

"Whoever you are, get off this frequency," snapped Henry. "This is strictly for police business."

"Henry, this is Mayor Turner and this *is* police business. I need you at Alsop's Bakery. *Now.* Do you copy?"

"I copy."

"Over and out," said Peggy. She went back to the bakery to wait for Henry. While she waited, she left a message for Chuck at the high school, then called Bob at the gas station.

Bob arrived before Henry.

"Bob, Papa Luigi is missing." Peggy turned to Gina. "When did you see him last?"

"Last night when I took him his supper. Maria had too much homework, so I went in her place."

"How was he then?"

"Distracted," said Gina. "I could tell he wanted me to leave. So, I left his food, kissed him goodnight, and said I'd see him this morning."

"Did you talk to him after that?"

"No. I went home, helped Maria with her homework, we had dinner, and went to bed early."

"I'll round up the guys from the volunteer firefighters," said Bob. "We'll start looking immediately. Don't worry, Gina. We'll find Papa Luigi before dark."

Henry parked the cruiser in front of the police station, then crossed the street to the bakery. "What's the emergency?"

"You took your own sweet time getting here," said Peggy. "I've already briefed Bob. Papa Luigi is missing. The volunteer firefighters are going to organize a search party. I'll stay here at the bakery with Gina."

Peggy looked at the bakery wall. There

was a framed photograph of Papa Luigi standing behind the pastry case, his face clearly visible.

"Gina, I need to borrow that picture," said Peggy, standing on tiptoe to take it off the wall. "Henry, take this photo and having a missing-person poster printed and hung every place you can think of in Cobb's Landing and the surrounding towns, including Grover's Corners. Don't forget to return the original."

Henry grabbed the framed photo. He was tempted to put Peggy in her place for treating him like a gofer, but realized that after the earlier events at Max's hotel, he wasn't in a position to push his luck. That thought rankled. Once the old man was found, Henry would get his life shipshape again.

At noon, Peggy went back to Tom's Tools to leave a note on the front door for Nicky, saying she was at the bakery. Pie yowled from inside her carrier when Peggy opened the front door. Peggy was horrified that in the confusion of the morning she'd forgotten all about the poor cat. She grabbed the carrier, drove home, and let Pie out to spend the afternoon napping on the living room sofa.

At the bakery there was no news of Papa

94

Luigi. With the time change the previous weekend, it would be completely dark on Main Street by six.

And darker still in the dense woods on the moonless night that was fast approaching.

Chapter 14

Peggy got home just before six and began rooting in her freezer, like a blind pig nosing for a truffle, looking for something — anything — to fix for dinner. But all she unearthed were UFO's. Unidentified frozen objects.

Nicky called down from his room. "Mom, Ian's at the front door."

Peggy had completely forgotten that Ian was bringing dinner. She ran to open the door.

Ian was loaded down with foil-wrapped containers. "Dinner is on Max. He tried to deliver your breakfast this morning, but you were never at the hardware store. This is what the guests at the hotel are eating tonight."

Peggy set the table while Ian put the food into serving dishes.

Nicky bounded into the kitchen. He flashed his palms at Peggy to show he'd washed his hands, high-fived Ian, then sat down at the table.

"Nicky, I've got some stamps for your collection," said Ian. "After dinner, we can put them in your album."

"That's super. Thanks, Ian."

"Max is really the one you should thank. Max gets mail from all over the world, and he's been saving the stamps for you."

After dinner, Peggy cleaned up the kitchen while Ian went to get the stamps for Nicky.

Peggy was just finishing the dishes, when Lavinia popped in the kitchen door.

"I had to put in overtime at the hospital today, and I just heard about Papa Luigi," said Lavinia. "Is there any news?"

Peggy shook her head.

"Oh, that poor man. I pray his cold doesn't get any worse," said Lavinia. She sniffed the air. "Something really smells good in here. What did you have for dinner tonight?"

"Beef Stroganoff," said Peggy. "It was delicious."

"Really? That makes my mouth water. Have you got any leftovers? Chuck had a quick bite with Charlie, then went back to Bob's. Charlie's in his room doing his homework, and I don't feel like cooking."

Peggy pointed to the refrigerator. "Help yourself. I just put it away, so it should only take a few seconds in the microwave to reheat."

Ian walked into the kitchen to refill his coffee cup, startling Lavinia.

"Ian. My God. Hi. I'm so embarrassed," said Lavinia. "PJ, why didn't you tell me Ian was here?"

Peggy smiled. "You haven't let me say much since you walked in the door."

"Good to see you, Lavinia," Ian said with a smile.

"PJ, I'll go home. We'll talk tomorrow." Lavinia headed for the kitchen door.

"Lovey, don't be an idiot," said Peggy. "Make yourself something to eat and sit down. Dinner tonight was Max's treat and there's plenty. Have some salad, too. Max's chef makes his bleu cheese dressing from scratch."

"Since when did Max go into the catering business?" Lavinia asked between bites. "He can send dinner to my house every night."

"Lovey, you didn't hear about Buddy?" asked Peggy.

"Buddy?" Lavinia poured more dressing on her salad. "Not again. When?"

"This morning," replied Peggy.

"Where was he this time?"

"Face down on the waterwheel."

Lavinia's fork was suspended in mid-air. "You have got to be kidding me. The waterwheel?"

"What goes around, comes around," said Ian.

Peggy kicked him under the table.

"And this time Max caught the perp in the act," said Peggy.

Lavinia put down her fork. "Who was it?"

"Roger Cartwright."

"Henry and Carole Ann's kid?" Lavinia pushed her plate aside. "Tell me everything."

Peggy turned to Ian. "Where's Nicky?"

"Upstairs doing his homework," replied Ian. "I told him we'd look at the stamps after he got his homework done."

"Uh-huh," said Peggy. "Nicky's probably talking to Charlie on his walkie-talkie. I'll bet they're playing computer games."

"Or cruising the Internet," said Ian.

"Not in this house," said Peggy. "We only have one phone line, and there's no extension in Nicky's room."

"Same thing in our house," said Lavinia. "I read in the paper about a kid who ran up a fifty-thousand dollar bill on his parents' credit card surfing the Net. I love Charlie to pieces, but if he pulled a stunt like that he'd be pounding rocks for the rest of his life to pay off that debt. Some parents have no control over their kids." She took another bite of Stroganoff. "Tell me about Roger Cartwright."

"Was it Chuck who said Roger acted like a member of Hell's Angels?" asked Peggy.

"I think so," said Lavinia.

"The kid sure looks the part," said Peggy. "He's got the Marlon Brando sneer down pat. And the black leather clothing. But I don't remember Brando having his eyebrow and tongue pierced."

"Really?"

Peggy nodded. "I saw it myself."

"That's gross," said Lavinia. "I'm surprised Henry and Carole Ann let him do it."

"I don't think they have much control over their son," said Ian.

That statement got Peggy's attention. "Is this fact or are you guessing?" she asked.

"A little of each," said Ian. "Roger is only seventeen, but he has quite a juvie record."

"I thought juvenile records were sealed," said Lavinia.

"They are," said Ian. "But Max has ways of getting information."

"I don't think Roger's background came

up when we interviewed Henry," said Lavinia.

"I know it didn't," said Peggy. "That I would have remembered. I do remember that on Henry's application he seemed to have changed jobs rather frequently in the past five years, never staying in one place more than a year."

"That would tally with when Roger began getting into trouble," said Ian.

"What sort of trouble?" asked Peggy.

"I'm not exactly sure," said Ian, "but it appears to have been serious enough to put him into juvenile detention."

"There but for the grace of God," said Lavinia. "It isn't easy being a parent." She stood up and took her dishes to the sink. "Thanks for dinner, PJ. Good to see you, Ian. I'm going home to call Gina and give her some moral support. I'll let you know if there's any news." Lavinia let herself out.

"Alone at last," said Ian, reaching for Peggy's hand.

Peggy frowned, pulling her hand away to tap her fingers on the table. "Something's bothering me."

"What?"

"If — and this is pure speculation — Roger was the one responsible for all three of Buddy's appearances, how did Roger get into the science classroom? Milt Flask swears the room was locked when Buddy was taken the second and third times."

Ian looked puzzled. "Maybe he had a key."

"Milt has the only key to the science room." Peggy thought for a minute, then slapped her forehead. "What a dunce I am. Of course Roger had a key. Henry's key. For security reasons, Henry has a copy of the master key to the high school. It unlocks every door in the school." Peggy shook her head slowly. "What am I going to do? We never had these problems when Stu McIntyre was the police chief." She looked at the clock, then reached for the phone. "Henry? Mayor Turner. I need your security keys. All of them. I'll be at your house in five minutes." Peggy hung up and turned to Ian. "Do me a favor? Stay with Nicky until I get back?"

Peggy returned with a large ring of keys to find Ian and Nicky sitting at the kitchen table looking at Nicky's stamp collection.

Ian was holding part of an envelope with his fingertips. "Where did you get these stamps, Nicky?"

"Aren't they cool? Maria gave them to me. She said they're from Nigeria."

"What would Maria be doing with

stamps from Nigeria?" asked Peggy, looking at the stamps over Ian's shoulder. "Her father is stationed in Iraq."

"They aren't from Maria's father," said Nicky. "Maria said Papa Luigi gave them to her. He gives Maria lots of stuff."

"Nicky, would you mind if I borrowed these stamps?" asked Ian. "I'll take special care of them, and you will get them back. That's a promise."

Nicky hesitated. "Well. Okay. If you promise to give them back."

"I promise, Nicky." Ian turned to Peggy. "Have you got a plastic bag?"

Peggy opened a kitchen drawer and held up a box of snack-sized Baggies. "This size okay?"

"Perfect." Ian slipped the portion of the envelope into the bag and sealed it shut. "I hate to eat and run, but I know this is a school night. I will return your stamps, Nicky. You can count on it."

Peggy walked Ian to the front door. "Thanks for dinner."

"Thank Max, it was his idea."

Peggy swallowed hard then broached the topic that had been on her mind all evening. "What is Missy doing in Cobb's Landing?"

Ian hesitated for a fraction of a second

then quickly replied, "She's here on business."

"What kind of business?"

"I'm not at liberty to divulge that information."

Peggy looked at Ian for a long moment. "Let's get something very clear," she said, "if Missy pulls any crap during her stay in Cobb's Landing, I personally will ride her out of town on a rail."

Ian left without kissing Peggy goodnight.

Chapter 15

At dawn, the volunteer firefighters resumed their search for Papa Luigi. They all wore heavy jackets to ward off the bone-chilling damp cold that had settled over Cobb's Landing, creating pockets of mist in the woods.

Peggy called Gina at seven. "I'm driving Nicky to school this morning. Why don't I stop and pick up Maria. It'll save you a trip. I know you want to stay close to the phone."

"I was thinking of keeping Maria home today," said Gina. "She's very upset over her grandfather's disappearance."

"I think a day at school might be the best thing for Maria," replied Peggy. "It's Halloween. Papa Luigi wouldn't want Maria to miss all the fun."

Gina hesitated.

"I'll be at your house shortly," said Peggy, hanging up the phone before Gina could change her mind.

"Good thinking, Peggy," said Lavinia,

who had come over in her robe and slippers to borrow some milk for Charlie's breakfast. "I like Gina, and I understand what she's going through. But she's far too dependent on Maria. She'll turn that girl into a nervous wreck." Lavinia took a quart of milk from Peggy's refrigerator and went back to her own kitchen, saying as she left, "I'll meet you at the hardware store at three."

Peggy called up the stairs. "Nicky, get a move on. Your breakfast is ready. We're picking up Maria to take her to school."

The mere mention of Maria's name acted on Nicky like a can of spinach on Popeye. Before Peggy could count to ten, Nicky was at the kitchen table wolfing down his breakfast.

Peggy dropped the kids at school and headed for the hardware store. After spending the previous day at the bakery with Gina, Peggy was a day behind. She still had to put together her costume for Halloween.

Ian called Peggy late in the morning. "Tell Nicky I need to keep his stamps another day. They're being looked at by a philatelist friend in Boston. He thinks the stamps may be counterfeit."

"Counterfeit? Nicky will be so disappointed."

"Don't say anything to Nicky until I know for sure."

Lavinia made her grand entrance at three on the dot. "How do I look?" She twirled so Peggy could get the full effect.

"Carolyn Jones and Cassandra Peterson eat your hearts out," said Peggy. "Lovey, you look absolutely bewitching. Has Chuck seen your costume?"

"Not yet. He was going directly to the haunted house from school. I think I'll go over there and surprise him. I'll be back to help you with trick or treat. You'd better get changed, PJ, the kids will be here any minute." Lavinia sailed out the door, Morticia Addams down to her distinctive walk.

Peggy went into the storeroom to change out of her Colonial Village garb and emerged as Count Dracula.

"Trick or treat!"

Peggy dropped packets of candy corn into outstretched trick or treat bags. Main Street was filled with witches, ghosts, goblins, cowboys, ballerinas, devils, and pumpkins, all calling "trick or treat" as they ran from shop to shop before going to the town square to parade before the judges of the costume contest. Max's horse-drawn buggies clip-clopped up Main Street between the square and the haunted house.

"Trick or treat!"

Peggy looked down at the *Star Wars* trio. "You three look great! Where are you going now?"

"The haunted house."

"Have fun, kids. Nicky, be back here by six. I've got your pumpkin ready for the pumpkin float. We'll all go together, okay?"

"Okay, Mom. You look awesome!" The *Star Wars* trio ran to join the other revelers parading down Main Street.

"Trick or treat, Mayor!"

Peggy did a double take as she looked at a mirror image of her own mask and costume. "Max?"

"Shhh." Max held a finger to his lips. He helped himself to candy corn, slipping it into a slash pocket in the red satin lining of his black cape. With a wink and a wave, Max was gone.

"Trick or treat!"

A tall nun and a shorter monk in a cowl stood in front of Peggy with outstretched hands. The monk maintained a vow of silence, but there was something very familiar about the nun's voice.

A gaggle of school children dressed as

ghosts flocked into Tom's Tools. The nun and monk slipped out the front door before Peggy could positively identify the nun's voice.

Peggy was down to her last box of candy corn when Lavinia reappeared. "PJ?"

Peggy dipped her head in a little bow.

"Great costume!" said Lavinia. "For a minute I thought Buddy had risen from the dead. Sorry I wasn't here to help you, but they needed me at the haunted house. Bob is still out looking for Papa Luigi, so I took tickets at the front door. It was a madhouse."

"There's still no sign of Papa Luigi?"

"Not a trace. It's as if the earth swallowed him whole."

The *Star Wars* trio trooped into Tom's Tools, their candy sacks bulging. "Look what we got, Mom!"

"Why don't you leave your candy here, and we'll pick it up later. It's time for the pumpkin float."

"Charlie, I've got your pumpkin in my car," said Lavinia.

"Maria, do you have a pumpkin?" asked Peggy.

Maria shook her head. "Papa Luigi was going to carve one for me. I guess he forgot."

"Here. Take mine." Peggy put the pumpkin with Missy's caricature carved on it into Maria's hands. "Nicky, here's yours." Nicky grinned as he looked at the Darth Vader face Peggy had made on his pumpkin. "Cool, Mom."

"I've got candles and matches in my bag," said Peggy. "Let's go down to the river."

The banks of the Rock River were packed with residents and tourists waiting for the pumpkin float to begin. The judges were standing on the narrow balcony on the second floor of the former button factory where they had the best view of the downstream finish line.

Never one to pass up a moneymaking opportunity, Max had set up a stand next to the hotel where carved pumpkins were selling for ten dollars each. Damn, thought Peggy, I wish I'd thought of that.

Before every race, each pumpkin was numbered on the back in fluorescent paint.

Peggy inserted fat white candles into Nicky's and Maria's pumpkins. "We'll light the candles just before you put the pumpkins in the river."

The younger children were already lined up to float their pumpkins.

One by one the candlelit pumpkins were put into the river where they bobbed like corks until they were caught in the current and swiftly traveled downstream. The spectators began yelling out numbers as if they were cheering on favorites at the Kentucky Derby. "Go, seventeen!" "Thirteen just sideswiped number nine." There were groans when a favorite capsized.

Chuck arrived from the haunted house with his carved pumpkin cradled in his arms. "Where's Peggy?"

"Right here, Chuck."

Chuck looked twice. "Didn't I just see you on the balcony with the judges?"

Peggy smiled but kept mum on the identity of her costumed twin.

"I'm ready to take you on, Peggy Jean."

Peggy laughed when she got a good look at Chuck's costume and slicked-down hair. "Are you going to tango with Morticia at the school dance?"

Chuck made a face. "I told Lavinia I'd dress the part, but that's as far as I was going. Let me see your pumpkin."

"How can I compete with that?" Peggy said, pointing at Chuck's pumpkin. "You put wings on it? I don't think that's in the rules."

"It's a vampire bat," said Chuck. "The wings are made of pumpkin, it's allowed."

The *Star Wars* trio lined up to float their pumpkins. Peggy lit the candles, and soon the pumpkins were bobbing in the river. Maria's was number thirty-seven.

"Go, thirty-seven!" Peggy yelled when the pumpkin caught a rogue current close to the river bank and nosed ahead of the competition.

Maria jumped up and down as she watched her pumpkin cross the finish line first. "I'm going to go get it," said Maria, "I want to take it home with me to show mama."

"Be careful, Maria. Wait, I'll go with you."

Peggy and Maria made their way through the crowd on the river bank. A few yards past the finish line, the river gently curved and slowed as the large rocks which gave the river its name impeded the forward rush of water.

There were pumpkins everywhere. Some looked like orange heads bobbing in the water, eerily lit from within. Some were caught in the rocks, the candle flames extinguished when the river water splashed inside. Some had met their demise on the river bank. One or two pumpkins were small enough to skim over the rocks and continued to float downstream.

But number thirty-seven was nowhere to be seen. It had vanished into thin air.

Chapter 16

Lavinia asked Chuck to take the *Star Wars* trio to the school dance. "Peggy and I are going back to the store to pick up the trick or treat bags. We'll meet you at the dance."

Chuck was still celebrating his win in the adult pumpkin float. Both Chuck and Maria had pinned their blue ribbons to the front of their costumes.

Peggy parked around the corner from old Mrs. McIntyre's house. Morticia and the count silently approached the house on foot. All the lights were out except for a badly carved pumpkin glowing on the front porch.

After they'd wrapped all the bushes in toilet paper, they yelled "trick or treat" and ran back to Peggy's car.

Lavinia collapsed with laughter. "Oh, I've wanted to do that again ever since high school. Too bad Stu isn't here to appreciate it."

Peggy started the car for a swift getaway. "Stu didn't think it was funny the first time. He had to clean up the mess and missed the championship football game. Remember?"

Lavinia continued laughing. "Admit it, PJ, you loved doing it."

"You're right, Lovey. But we can't tell anyone. Especially our kids. We're supposed to be setting a good example."

"Oh, stuff it, PJ. It's Halloween, it was a bit of harmless fun. Don't you remember our parents telling us about the stuff they did on Halloween? Soaping windows, pelting people with water balloons and bags full of flour."

When they walked into the school auditorium, one of the first people they saw was old Mrs. McIntyre, dressed as Glenda, the Good Witch of the North.

"Right movie, wrong witch," whispered Peggy.

Lavinia snorted to cover her laughter. "C'mon, let's get some punch. I'm parched."

They made their way across the dance floor where ghosts, ghouls, witches, and goblins were gyrating to the strains of "Monster Mash" performed by the high school band. At the refreshment table a witch ladled punch from a black cauldron into paper cups.

"Did you get my candy, Mom?"

"It's in Peggy's car, Charlie. You can have it when we get home. Where's your father?"

Charlie gestured to a spot across the room. "He's over there, someplace."

Lavinia slithered off to find Chuck.

"Where are Nicky and Maria?" asked Peggy.

"I dunno." Charlie made a face. "I think they're dancing."

Peggy tossed her empty punch cup in the trash bin. "Come on, Charlie. I'll dance with you. We'll find Nicky and Maria, and you can cut in."

"Cut in? What's that?"

How times have changed, Peggy thought. She remembered the Halloween dances when she was in school. When the band played real music. Peggy shook her head. Lavinia's right, she thought. I am becoming an old poop stick-in-the-mud. She turned to Charlie. "Cutting in is something they did in old movies."

They found Nicky and Maria sitting on the sidelines, looking shy and awkward. "I thought you two were dancing," said Peggy. Then she realized that Nicky and Charlie didn't know how to dance. They were two eleven-year-old boys who had spent most of their free time at the base-ball field or playing catch in their back-yards. "Come on, guys — you, too Maria — we're all going to dance together. It's easy. Watch me and do what I do." Peggy began to move with the strong beat of the music, and soon the four of them were dancing and having a good time. They weren't the most polished group on the dance floor, but they were the most enthusiastic.

The music changed to a slow number and the *Star Wars* trio headed off to the refreshment table. The tall nun approached Peggy. " 'Is it real or is it Memorex?' "

"What?"

"May I have this dance?"

Peggy and Ian moved smoothly together around the dance floor.

"It's pretty funny that you and Max picked the same costume," said Ian.

"I put mine off until the last minute," said Peggy. "Where is Max? Is he here?"

"I haven't seen him since the pumpkin float," said Ian. "Halloween is a very busy night for Max. He's in great demand in a number of places."

"Like where?" asked Peggy.

"You know I can't tell you that," said Ian.

"You can't, or you won't?"

"I really couldn't say," replied Ian.

Peggy spotted someone in a Freddy costume talking to Morticia and Gomez. "I think that's Bob. I want to talk to him." The nun and the count danced their way across the floor.

"Bob, is that you?" asked Peggy.

"Peggy?"

Peggy nodded.

"Who's that?" asked Lavinia, nodding in the tall nun's direction.

The nun moved silently away from the group.

"Where are the kids?"

"They're at the refreshment table, Lovey." Peggy turned to Bob. "Is there any news of Papa Luigi?"

Bob shook his head. "Peggy, we've looked everywhere. It's been almost forty-eight hours since anyone's seen him. It's time to call the county police, or maybe the National Guard."

"I'll take care of it," said Peggy. "I know Gina is grateful for all you and the firefighters have done."

"It's the least we can do for Lew," said Bob.

Peggy caught sight of the monk in the cowl whispering to Ian. He listened intently, then — to Peggy's increasing irritation — they left together arm in arm.

The school dance ended at ten. By eleven Nicky had gorged himself with candy and was complaining of a stomachache. Peggy gave him some Alka-Seltzer to calm his stomach and sent him to bed.

She sat alone in her kitchen drinking a cup of hot cocoa laced with a dollop of brandy.

Lavinia tapped on the back door. "I saw your light on. Everyone's asleep in my house. What are you drinking?" She reached for Peggy's cup and took a sip. "Oh, that's good."

Peggy got a clean mug for Lavinia. The two women sat with their feet up, drinking cocoa.

"I thought today went pretty well," said Lavinia, pouring more cocoa in her cup.

Peggy nodded, the brandy was making her sleepy.

"Where did you and Maria go during the pumpkin float?"

"We tried to find her pumpkin. She wanted to show it to Gina."

"What happened to it?"

"I don't know. But tomorrow morning I'm going to find out. You want to come with me?"

"Sure." Lavinia put down her cup and yawned. "I'm beat. See you in the morning." At the doorway, she turned back to Peggy and said, "The next time you see Ian, tell him he's the best-looking nun I've ever seen." With a whoop of laughter, Lavinia closed the door and crossed into her own backyard.

Chapter 17

All Saints' Day dawned cold and damp. Peggy reluctantly hauled herself out of bed and went to the kitchen to make a pot of coffee. While it was perking, she placed a call to the county police.

"It's been more than forty-eight hours since anyone has seen Papa Luigi," she said. "The volunteer fire department has searched the area extensively and found nothing. They're exhausted. We need help."

She made a face at the phone while she listened. "I know you're understaffed, but so are we. We have one police officer in Cobb's Landing. Henry Cartwright. But he's been here only a few months and doesn't know the area." Peggy bit her tongue. "Do what you can. I'll be at the hardware store later. Thanks."

Peggy hung up, muttering "thanks for nothing" under her breath, then dialed another number. No answer. As she looked out her kitchen window at the steady drizzle, she spotted Lavinia in her own kitchen. Peggy held up an empty coffee cup; Lavinia smiled and held up her hand, fingers spread. Five minutes.

Lavinia wrapped her hands around the warm coffee cup. "You really want to go out in this slop looking for a pumpkin?"

From the look on Lavinia's face, Peggy knew her friend was thinking "are you nuts?" but wasn't saying it aloud.

"I'm not as gung ho as I was last night," Peggy admitted, "but I promised Maria."

"Is there any news of Papa Luigi?"

Peggy shook her head. "I called the county for help. All I got was crabbing about how understaffed they are. I called Henry Cartwright but there's no answer at his house. That man is useless. I think he spends more time pressing his uniform than he does on police business. But Henry is all we've got. I don't think the county did us any favors when they sent him to Cobb's Landing."

"Makes you wish we still had Stu around."

Peggy nodded. Being the mayor of a small town wasn't all ribbon cutting and pumpkin floats.

"Chuck and Charlie are watching Saturday morning cartoons. Leave a note for

122

Nicky. He can have breakfast at our house. I'll meet you out front in ten minutes."

Peggy put on knee-high rubber boots and her hooded yellow slicker over her jeans and thick sweater. She stuffed a pair of gloves in her slicker pocket.

Lavinia was sporting a bright orange rain poncho over her jeans and jacket. On her feet were tennis shoes. "You're really serious about this," she said as she eyed Peggy's boots. "We're going to need something to warm us after being out in this slop. I'll treat to coffee and muffins at Clemmie's."

The two women walked gingerly on sidewalks covered with rain-slicked leaves as they headed over to Main Street. The time/temperature sign at the Citizen's Bank showed the current temperature to be forty-one degrees, a damp chill that ate through clothing into your bones. The windows of Clemmie's Cafe were brightly lit and inviting.

Lavinia slowed her pace when she spotted Bob, Slim, and the boys inside having coffee in their favorite booth. Peggy tugged at Lavinia's sleeve. "Later, Lovey."

"Hey, you two." Bob stuck his head out of Clemmie's front door. "Where you headed?"

"On a fool's errand," Lavinia replied. "Peggy's looking for a pumpkin."

"Seems a right fool thing to do on a rainy morning." Bob ducked back into Clemmie's.

They walked down to the Rock River. Fragrant wood smoke curled skyward from the chimney at the former button factory. Peggy made a mental note to stock up on wood for the coming winter for her own fireplace.

Along the river bank, skeletal tree limbs were silhouetted black against the gray sky. A few maple leaves clung stubbornly to the branches providing a splash of color in the bleak late fall landscape.

"It's reminds me of a story we read in high school English class," remarked Lavinia. "About a woman who looked at a tree outside her bedroom window, and the leaf that stayed on the tree all winter."

" 'The Last Leaf' " said Peggy. "O. Henry wrote it. I've got it in a book at home."

"I liked that story," said Lavinia. "I think I'll read it again this weekend." Lavinia grinned. "At your house."

The two women walked single-file along the river bank path, Peggy in the lead. They reached the curve in the river where Peggy had been with Maria the night before.

Lavinia looked down at her feet. Water was lapping against the thick soles of her tennis shoes. She quickly moved a couple of steps upland. "How odd. The river looks wider today," said Lavinia. "We haven't had that much rain since last night."

The floating pumpkins had piled up against the rocks creating a temporary dam. A shallow rivulet carried the overflow off to the right into the dense woods.

"It was too dark last night to see this. I'm going to find out where the water goes," said Peggy, stepping into water up to her ankles. Her feet were warm and dry inside her wool socks and rubber boots.

"You were the smart one to wear boots," said Lavinia. "I'll stay right here on dry land. Don't be too long. I'm getting cold."

Peggy paused to put on her gloves, then began trudging downstream into the woods, using her hands to push away branches and bushes. Bits and pieces of pumpkin, like the breadcrumbs Hansel and Gretel dropped to find their way home, created a path for Peggy to follow. The water grew shallower as she went deeper into the woods.

She had traveled less than a quarter mile through the hilly countryside when she spied a bright orange object ahead of her.

Nestled against a tree trunk was the pumpkin bearing Missy's face.

"Mystery solved!" Peggy exclaimed aloud as she examined the pumpkin. She turned it around. On the back was painted the number *thirty-seven*.

As she bent down to pick up the pumpkin, she heard a sound. She cocked her head and listened, mentally filtering out the woodland noises of twittering birds and creaking branches. Then she heard it again. A sound like a low moan.

But where was it coming from?

Peggy stood rooted to her spot at the tree. She dropped the hood of her slicker to her shoulders and slowly turned her head.

She heard the sound a third time. Coming from her left. She looked and saw a thick clump of bushes on the hillside. She went toward the bushes and heard the sound again. Louder.

Peggy pushed her way through the bushes into a small cave. Although there was space to stand upright, in width there was barely enough room to swing a cat.

Lying on the ground inside the cave were two figures.

One was Papa Luigi. His arms were crossed over his chest as he hugged himself for warmth, his feet were bound with rope. Peggy touched his forehead. He was still alive, but burning with fever, his breath was ragged and thick. His sporadic moans echoed in the small enclosed space.

Lying on its back was a second figure, dressed as Count Dracula. The figure was motionless.

Next to Papa Luigi was a gun.

Peggy bolted out of the cave and ran back to the river bank.

Chapter 18

Lavinia was hopping from one foot to the other. "What took you so long, PJ? I'm freezing. Let's go to Clemmie's for coffee."

"Lovey, I found Papa Luigi. Run to the inn and call for help. We need an ambulance fast."

"You found him? He's alive?"

"He's alive, but he's burning up with fever. Hurry. I'll wait right here."

While Peggy waited, she thought about the figure in the Count Dracula costume. She prayed it was Buddy, but feared it was Max and was surprised to find her eyes filling with tears.

Lavinia was back in less than five minutes. "I called Bob at Clemmie's. He's on the way in his truck. We'll meet the ambulance."

"Lovey, run back to the inn for blankets. We'll need them for makeshift stretchers. I don't think Papa Luigi can walk."

Lavinia returned with Bob, Slim, and Chuck and an armload of blankets. Peggy led the way through the woods to the cave entrance.

Bob let out a low whistle. "I've lived in Cobb's Landing all my life, but I never knew this cave was here. Did anyone?"

They all shook their heads.

The cave was too small for everyone to enter. Peggy and Lavinia went inside with blankets.

"My God," said Lavinia, looking at the figure in the Count Dracula costume. "Who's that?"

"It's probably Buddy. Another Halloween prank. Let's take care of Papa Luigi first."

"Chuck, I need your knife," said Lavinia.

Chuck's arm poked through the bushes into the cave opening. In his hand was his prized possession, the mother of all Swiss Army Knives. Chuck often bragged he could build a house with that knife.

Lavinia quickly cut the ropes binding Papa Luigi's feet, then put her ear against his chest. "He's got pneumonia, PJ, and he's unconscious. We need to get him out of here fast."

They wrapped a blanket around Papa Luigi, then improvised a stretcher with two more blankets.

Bob and Slim carried Papa Luigi out of

the woods with Chuck as point man to clear the way.

Peggy moved to the Count Dracula figure. She carefully removed the mask from its face.

It wasn't Buddy, and it wasn't Max. Peggy was staring at the face of Roger Cartwright. If this was a Halloween prank, it was one that had gone sadly awry. Roger had been shot though the heart.

Chapter 19

Peggy stayed behind at the cave with Roger's body while Lavinia went to the inn to call Henry Cartwright and the medical examiner.

Lavinia and Chuck returned in half an hour with the medical examiner and a thermos of hot coffee.

"There was no answer at the Cartwright's," said Lavinia. "Papa Luigi is on the way to the hospital. Thank God the ambulance arrived at the inn in time. Otherwise Papa Luigi would have gone to the hospital in the cab of Bob's tow truck. I called Gina; she and Maria are heading for the hospital."

The medical examiner came out of the cave. "I'd say the victim has been dead for almost twelve hours. But it's difficult to be more accurate under these circumstances. I'll have a report for you early next week. Someone will have to make an official identification." He turned to Chuck. "I've bagged the body. Can you help me get it out of here?" Chuck nodded. The examiner turned back to Peggy. "Did you touch the weapon?" Peggy shook her head. "I'll bag it and take it with me. You need to get the police here for a more detailed investigation. I took some digital camera shots of the scene. They're welcome to them."

The last blanket became a makeshift bier for Roger Cartwright's body as the four-some made their way out of the woods, each clutching a corner of the blanket.

Peggy's pumpkin remained in place at the base of the tree to mark the position of the cave.

When they got to the inn, Lavinia ran inside to return the empty thermos.

"Did you see Max?" asked Peggy.

"No, I asked, but they said he hadn't been around since the pumpkin float. What do we do now, PJ?"

Peggy looked at Lavinia and Chuck. "We need to go to the Cartwright's. This isn't something I want to do alone. Then I'm going to take you up on that coffee and muffin at Clemmie's."

Carole Ann Cartwright answered the front door in her robe and slippers.

Peggy glanced at her watch, it was almost ten. Practically the middle of the afternoon for residents of Cobb's Landing. "I'm sorry to disturb you. May we come in?"

"I trust this won't take long," said Carole Ann.

"We'll wait in the car, Peggy." Lavinia and Chuck backed down the walkway.

"Is Henry at home?" asked Peggy. "I need to talk to both of you."

"He's upstairs," said Carole Ann. "I'll get him."

Henry Cartwright descended the stairs, tying the sash of his robe. "Is this visit really necessary?"

"I've been trying to call you," said Peggy.

"We had the phone unplugged," said Henry.

"Perhaps we'd better sit down." Peggy walked into the spotless living room. "This isn't easy for me to say." Peggy took a deep breath. "Your son is dead. His body was found this morning." She fumbled in her pocket. "The medical examiner will want you to identify the body. Here's his number." Peggy put a business card on the polished coffee table. "I'm truly sorry for your loss." Receiving no response, Peggy continued. "I'll let myself out. Please call me if there's anything I can do."

Pulling the Cartwright's front door shut

behind her, Peggy resisted the impulse to sprint to the sanctuary of the Coopers' car.

Once inside the car, Peggy exhaled for the first time since entering the Cartwright house. She glared at Chuck and Lavinia. "You two are lily-livered cowards! How could you leave me there all alone?"

"The Cartwrights' weren't prepared for visitors, and it seemed as if we were ganging up on them. Three against two," said Lavinia. "How did they take the news?"

"I think they were in a state of total shock," said Peggy. "Neither one of them said a word." Peggy sighed. "I know I handled it badly." Peggy sighed again.

"I'm sure you handled it just fine," said Lavinia. "You need coffee. Let's go to Clemmie's."

"I'll meet you there," said Peggy. "I need to stop at the hardware store and make some calls. Is Nicky at your house?"

"When I left, the boys were eating Pop-Tarts and watching cartoons," said Chuck. "Don't worry, PJ, they're fine."

For the second time that morning, Peggy called the county police. "I know you're short-staffed, but we need someone here in Cobb's Landing immediately. We found Papa Luigi this morning. He's in the hospital now with an acute case of pneumonia. He needs police protection. He may be the victim of a kidnapping." Then Peggy articulated the thought that had been in her mind since the first time she entered the cave. "He may also be a murder suspect. He was found next to the body of Roger Cartwright." Peggy listened for a moment. "Yes, you heard me correctly. Roger Cartwright. Henry's son. Roger is dead. You can call the medical examiner for details." Peggy listened again. "I agree. Considering the circumstances, Henry is not the proper person to be investigating this case. Let me know when I can expect his temporary replacement."

Chapter 20

The Cobb's Landing snoop sisters sprung into action.

"Okay, PJ, I'm ready. What have you got?"

"Two tuna-noodle casseroles. One for Gina and Maria, one for the Cartwrights."

"I made two batches of brownies. Let's roll. Chuck is playing cutthroat Monopoly with the boys at our house. They'll be at it all afternoon."

"This time you go into the Cartwrights', Lovey, and I'll wait in the car. You owe me for this morning."

They made the Cartwright house their first stop. Lavinia marched up to the door bearing the foil-wrapped containers of food. She tapped the polished brass knocker and waited. Carole Ann Cartwright answered the door, dressed in pressed slacks and sweatshirt. Peggy couldn't hear what Lavinia said, but she saw Carole Ann shake her head. Lavinia returned to the car, the food still in her hands.

"PJ, you're not going to believe this." Lavinia did her best to mimic Carole Ann. " 'We are vegetarians and we don't indulge in sweets.' " In her normal voice Lavinia added, "How ungrateful can anyone be?"

Peggy rolled her eyes. "Look at it this way, Lovey. We don't have to worry about what we're having for dinner tonight. We've got tuna casserole with brownies for dessert. We've got enough to feed the neighborhood."

The next stop was Gina's house on Elm Street. Gina's car was parked in the driveway. Lavinia held the food while Peggy tapped on the front door.

Gina opened the door. When she saw Peggy, Gina threw her arms around Peggy in a smothering hug. "Peggy." Tears flowed down Gina's cheeks onto Peggy's yellow rain slicker. "I will never be able to thank you for what you've done."

"It's only a casserole and brownies," said Lavinia.

Gina released Peggy. She reached in her pocket for a tissue to blow her nose. "It's been an emotional day. Please come in." She took the food from Lavinia. "We just got back from the hospital. I haven't given a thought to dinner. I really appreciate this. Thank you both."

"Don't mention it," said Lavinia, hoping to forestall the tears she saw welling once again in Gina's eyes. "How's Papa Luigi doing?"

"They've got him on oxygen and antibiotics. They would only let me stay in the room for a few minutes."

"I'll check with the doctor when I'm on duty and find out what's going on, Gina," said Lavinia. "Don't worry. Papa Luigi is getting the best of care."

"Have you two got time for coffee?" asked Gina.

"Love some," said Peggy.

They settled themselves in Gina's spacious kitchen, at a table flanked by French windows. Outside the windows were lilac bushes, dormant until spring when the scent of the blooming lavender flowers would fill the room.

Gina poured coffee and put out a plate of Halloween cookies. "These are the last for this year. Next week I'll start making cookies for Thanksgiving." She turned to Peggy. "Now I want to hear how you found Papa Luigi."

"Promise you won't start blubbering again, Gina," said Lavinia, reaching for a cookie.

Gina smiled wanly.

"Where's Maria?" asked Peggy.

"She's next door playing with her friend Michelle," said Gina. "Shall I get her?"

Peggy shook her head. "You can decide later how much you want Maria to know." Peggy recounted the story of the missing pumpkin from the pumpkin float and how searching for the pumpkin led her to Papa Luigi. "I don't know if anyone told you, Gina, but Papa Luigi wasn't alone in the cave."

Gina's eyes grew wide. "Who else was there?"

"Lying close to him was a figure dressed as Count Dracula," replied Peggy.

Gina put down her coffee cup. "Was it Buddy?"

"Not this time," said Peggy.

"Who was it?"

"Roger Cartwright."

"Henry and Carole Ann Cartwright's son? What was he doing there?"

"That's what we're trying to figure out."

"What does Roger say?"

"He's dead, Gina. Roger was shot. There was a gun on the ground next to Papa Luigi."

"So that's why the police came to the hospital," said Gina. "They arrived just as Maria and I were leaving."

"It's a bit more serious than that," said Peggy. "Papa Luigi may be a suspect in Roger's death."

Gina looked at Peggy and Lavinia. "You two have known Papa Luigi all your lives. I didn't meet him until Lew and I were planning to get married and I moved to Cobb's Landing. But I know this much about my father-in-law. Luigi Alsop wouldn't hurt a fly. He's spent his entire life caring for his family." Gina's back straightened and a determined look settled on her face. "I'm through blubbering." Gina smiled brightly at Lavinia, then turned to Peggy. "Tell me what I can do to help."

"I'd like to look around Papa Luigi's house," said Peggy. "Right now I can't think of any possible connection between Papa Luigi and Roger Cartwright. Can you?"

Gina shook her head. "What would they have in common?"

"Perhaps we'll find a link at Papa Luigi's," said Peggy.

Gina reached for her keys. "Let's go."

It didn't take long to reach Papa Luigi's house in Alsop's woods. They parked in the gravel drive and waited on the front porch while Gina fished for the door key on her key ring.

Gina flipped on the lights. The house was cold and devoid of human presence. It was tidy but felt empty, as if the owner had been away a long time. Lavinia turned up the thermostat on the furnace.

"Papa Luigi built this house right before Lew and I got married," said Gina. "By then, Lew's mother had passed away. Papa Luigi said the house in town was too big for him alone, but too small for the three of us. He gave the house on Elm Street to Lew and me for a wedding present and moved out here."

Papa Luigi's house in the woods was built on one level. Living room, wood-burning fireplace, kitchen with adjoining dining area, two bedrooms — one doubled as a study — and a full bath. In the second bedroom was a large rolltop desk.

Gina slid back the rolltop. Papa Luigi's papers were neatly organized in the pigeonholes. "I wouldn't know what to look for," said Gina.

"Would you mind if I had a look?" asked Peggy. "That is, if it wouldn't upset Papa Luigi. I promise I'll keep everything in order."

"Papa Luigi is a very private man, but if it'll clear him of any suspicion in Roger Cartwright's death, I'm sure it'll be all

141

right," said Gina. "I'll look around his bedroom."

"I'll check the living room and kitchen," said Lavinia.

Papa Luigi was also a methodical man. His bills were sorted by type and date of payment. Peggy moved on to the familiar brown envelopes that held the statements sent by the Citizen's Bank. She opened the most recent statement. Papa Luigi was by no means flush; there had been steady cash withdrawals from his account, in addition to the odd amounts deducted to cover the checks he'd written to pay his bills.

Gina popped her head in the doorway. "Did you find anything?"

"Did Papa Luigi usually walk around with large amounts of cash in his pocket?"

"Heavens no. He always said his needs were small; if he had enough cash to buy a newspaper or an ice cream cone for Maria, that was plenty. Why?"

Peggy held out the bank statement. "He's been taking large amounts of cash out of his account."

Gina scanned the statement. "This doesn't make sense. There must be some mistake. I'll take it up with the bank on Monday. I wonder how long he's been doing this?" Gina sat down with the packet of bank statements. After looking at the second statement, she got up and headed for the kitchen. "I don't know about anyone else, but I need a glass of Papa Luigi's homemade wine. Join me?"

"I'll have one," said Lavinia. "I haven't found a single thing. All I can say is Papa Luigi's kitchen is a lot neater than mine will ever be. He even alphabetizes his canned goods."

"Be there in a minute," said Peggy as she opened a narrow drawer in the desk.

Inside the drawer were several letters held together by a rubber band. The stamps were missing from the top envelope — the upper right portion of the envelope had been neatly cut away — but the remaining envelopes bore identical postage.

Peggy slid the single sheet out of the top envelope and began to read. Then she read the remaining letters. When she was finished, she walked into the living room where Gina and Lavinia were sipping wine.

"Gina, there's no mistake in those bank statements. I know where the cash went."

Chapter 21

Gina poured a glass of wine for Peggy.

Peggy took a generous sip, then another. "Listen to this." She began reading from the letter in her hand.

Good Day,

With warm hearts I offer my friend-ship and my greetings, and I hope this letter meets you in good time. It will be surprising to you to receive this pro-posal from me since you do not know me personally. However, I am sincerely seeking your confidence in this transac-tion, which I propose with my free mind and as a person of integrity.

The purpose of this letter is to seek your most needed assistance in a busi-ness venture. Due to the land and polit-ical reforms in Nigeria, all farmers were asked to surrender their farms to the government for redistribution.

When my father refused to surrender his farm, the police were ordered to invade my father's farm and burn down everything in the farm. They killed my father and took away a lot of items from his farm. After the death of my father, our local pastor and a close friend of my father handed us over his will documents with instructions from my father that we should leave Nigeria in case anything happened to him.

The will documents has a certificate of deposit, confirming a cash deposit totaling three million six hundred thousand United State dollars. Kept in custody for us in a security company unknown to the company that the content is money hence it was deposited as personal belongings. This money was deposited with this private security company for safety and security reasons.

This violent and barbaric act has since led to the death of my beloved mother and kid sister and other innocent lives. I was continually threatened to abandon my inheritance from my father after he was murdered. I resisted for a while, but when the danger became unbearable, and I survived two murder attempts, I find myself in need to leave Nigeria.

Therefore I must transfer this money to an account in your country. I am seeking a genuine and reliable partner, to whose account this money can be transferred, hence this proposal to you.

You have to understand that this decision taken by me is a very big and brave one, and it entrusts my future in your hands, as a result of the safe keeping of this money. The company will be legally informed of you representing me.

You will receive twenty-five percent of the money for your assistance, and helping me open an account for the money to be deposited in your country.

Please, I want you to maintain absolute secrecy for the purpose of this transaction. I look forward to your reply, and I thank you in advance as I anticipate your co-operation.

Sincerely Yours,

Peggy passed the rest of the letters to Gina, then sat back and drank her wine.

"I don't get it," said Lavinia. "How did Papa Luigi lose money if he was to get twenty-five percent of . . . how much?"

"Three million, six hundred thousand," said Peggy.

146

"Twenty-five percent of that is . . ." Lavinia did some quick math in her head. "Nine hundred thousand dollars. Hell, let's call it an even million. That's not chicken feed."

"You haven't read the rest of the letters," said Peggy. "There are expenses for getting the money out of Nigeria. Papa Luigi has been paying those expenses out of his own pocket."

"He'll get the money back, won't he?" asked Gina. "When he gets the million?"

"Gina," Peggy said gently, "I don't think there is any money in Nigeria. This smells like a scam. I'm afraid Papa Luigi is being taken for a ride."

Chapter 22

The empty tuna-casserole dish sat in the middle of Lavinia's kitchen table.

"Who wants dessert?" asked Lavinia.

"I do!" said Charlie.

"Me, too!" said Nicky.

"Wait a minute," said Peggy. "I've got an idea. Nicky, run home and get the vanilla ice cream out of the freezer, and the carton of eggs out of the refrigerator. You go, too, Charlie. You can carry the eggs. We're going to have something different for dessert tonight. It'll be like a science project."

"*Boring*, Mom," said Nicky.

"Just you wait, Nicky," said Peggy. "You're going to like this a lot."

Chuck and Lavinia cleared the table while Peggy got out large bowls and a hand-mixer to make dessert.

Nicky and Charlie came back with the ice cream and eggs. They were followed by Ian.

"Hope I'm not barging in," said Ian. "I've been calling since I got back from

Boston an hour ago, but there was never anyone home. When are you going to get an answering machine?"

"When pigs have wings," said Peggy, pointing at two mixing bowls. "Take off your jacket and start separating those eggs."

Ian looked at the eggs, the pan of brownies, and the ice cream. "Oh, you're making . . ."

Peggy clamped her hand over Ian's mouth. "It's a surprise. I told the boys it's a science project." She turned to Nicky and Charlie. "Remember when you were in first grade with Miss McNab?"

"She was a neat teacher," said Nicky.

"Yeah," said Charlie, "she made everything fun."

"And she never yelled at us," said Nicky.

"Or sent us to the principal's office," said Charlie.

"Do you remember your first science project?"

Nicky and Charlie looked at each other, then both shrugged and shook their heads.

"The project was to discover things that float."

"Oh, yeah," said Nicky, a big smile illuminating his face. "That was so cool. You filled up the bathtub and we dropped all kinds of things in it."

"Then you ran downstairs and got your Halloween pumpkin and dropped it in the tub. Remember how surprised you were?"

Lavinia laughed. "I'd forgotten that's how the pumpkin float originated. Nicky came over and got Charlie. They pedaled down to the river with their pumpkins in the baskets of their bikes."

"Then what happened?" asked Ian.

"The boys dropped their pumpkins in the river and watched them float away," said Lavinia. "Charlie was so upset about losing his pumpkin he told me a goblin took it."

"*Mother.*"

Lavinia ruffled Charlie's hair. She turned to Peggy. "All right, Mr. Wizard, what's tonight's lesson?"

"Mr. Wizard?" asked Chuck. "That brings back memories." He turned to his son. "It was a science program on television called *Ask Mr. Wizard.*"

"I know, Dad," said Charlie. "They show it on the Discovery science channel. It's in black-and-white like those dorky old movies you watch, Mom."

"Those old monster movies you watch are also in black-and-white," said Lavinia.

"Those are pretty cool," said Charlie.

"Tonight there's a triple monster feature for Halloween. Can I stay up and watch?"

"Me, too?" asked Nicky.

"Before you run off to watch the movies, we're going to learn about temperature and insulation," said Peggy. "What do you think happens to ice cream when you put it in the oven?"

"It melts and makes a big mess," said Nicky.

"Wait and see," said Peggy.

Ian finished separating the eggs. Peggy began making a meringue. Nicky and Charlie scooped the vanilla ice cream onto the pan of brownies. Peggy quickly spread the meringue over the ice cream. "You want to make sure every bit of ice cream is covered all the way to the edge of the pan." She popped the pan into the oven under the broiler. "Now watch what happens."

Three minutes later, the meringue nicely browned, she took the pan from the oven and began cutting portions to put on plates.

"The ice cream didn't melt," said Nicky. He dug in with his spoon. "This stuff is great."

"It's called Baked Alaska," said Ian, finishing his own serving. He turned to Peggy. "Thank you. It was delicious."

151

"Lavinia made the brownies."

"They were excellent." A car horn tooted. "I really can't stay. I came to return Nicky's stamps." Ian handed a small brown envelope to Nicky. "I'm afraid I have bad news. They're counterfeit. Even though they're useless as postage, I'd hang on to them, Nicky. Sometimes you can learn more from fakes than the real thing."

"I'll see you out," said Peggy. She walked with Ian to the Cooper's front door. When she got back to the kitchen, Charlie and Nicky were gone.

"Where did the boys go?"

"They're over at your house watching monstermania on TV," said Lavinia. "Send Charlie home when you're ready to go to bed."

"Why doesn't Charlie spend the night at our house?" asked Peggy. "I'll make breakfast for the boys in the morning, and you can sleep in."

"It's football for me," said Chuck, heading for the living room.

Peggy began washing the dessert dishes.

"Stop that," said Lavinia. "I'll do them later."

"I made the mess," said Peggy, "I'll do the cleanup."

Lavinia picked up a dish towel and

began drying. "You want to tell me what's going on with you and Ian?"

"Apparently nothing," said Peggy. "Ever since Missy came back, he's been distant and secretive. That was her car parked out front."

"Oh, crap," said Lavinia. "PJ, I'm really sorry."

"I'm not sure I am," said Peggy.

"Really?"

"Really. Let's talk about something else," said Peggy.

"Okay. What stamps was Ian talking about?"

"Stamps?"

"The ones he gave back to Nicky."

"Oh, those."

"Earth to Peggy," said Lavinia. "I know it's been a long day, but did you leave your brain in the woods?"

"No, I just thought of something. Where are those letters Papa Luigi received?"

"Gina has them. Why?"

"I think Nicky's stamps came from the first letter." Peggy wiped her hands on the towel Lavinia was holding. "Put on a pot of coffee, Lovey, I'll be right back."

Peggy returned with the small brown envelope and a large magnifying glass.

Lavinia poured coffee and the two

women settled in at the Cooper's kitchen table. It was the same round, golden oak table where Peggy and Lavinia had sat with their coloring books as children, later their school books, and later still to address the invitations for their weddings. It was as familiar to them as the table in Peggy's own kitchen. Over the years, the kitchens in both houses had been repainted, repapered, appliances replaced, and floors recovered, but the golden oak tables and pressed-back chairs remained the same.

Peggy opened the small brown envelope. Inside was the plastic snack-sized Baggie she'd given to Ian sandwiched between two pieces of cardboard. Inside the Baggie was a portion of an envelope bearing postage.

"PJ, take it out of the bag so we can get a better look."

Peggy shook her head. "I don't think we should, Lovey. We did something incredibly stupid this afternoon by getting our fingerprints all over Papa Luigi's letters."

"With the letters it's you, me, Gina, Papa Luigi, and the person who sent the letters. Who knows how many people have handled the stamps? Go on, open the bag."

"Oh, all right." Peggy opened the bag. They looked at the fragment of the envelope. On the upper portion of the stamp

154

were the words *Nigeria, N50;* underneath the denomination was printed "Rock Bridge." The words were in yellow against a black background. The depicted bridge had a reddish hue.

"Rock Bridge?" said Lavinia. "That's pretty ironic, don't you think?"

"I think whoever prints the stamps in Nigeria needs a better printer; this really looks crappy. It's all fuzzy."

"What do you expect, PJ? Ian said it was counterfeit. How did Nicky get this stamp?"

"From Maria. He said she gave it to him."

"And she got it from Papa Luigi?"

"That's what Nicky said."

"Don't tell Charlie," said Lavinia.

"Why not?" said Peggy.

Lavinia smiled. "I think Charlie's got a crush on Maria."

Peggy sighed.

"What's the matter, PJ?"

"I think Nicky also has a crush on Maria."

The two mothers sighed.

"Our boys are growing up, Lovey."

They sighed again.

"What are we going to do about it, PJ?"

"There's nothing we can do, Lovey."

"I meant about Maria."

"The boys will work it out for themselves. Remember that summer we both had a crush on . . ." Peggy thought for a minute. "Funny, I can't remember his name."

"I know who you mean. The boy who spent the summer here. His grandparents lived across the street. You and I used to hide in our rooms and spy on him. He sure was cute."

"We got over it, Lovey. And we're still friends. The boys will work it out."

"I suppose so. But they're so young."

Peggy laughed. "We can't have it both ways, Lovey. One minute they're growing up too fast, then they're so young. Actually, they're almost the same age we were that summer."

"Bobby Gibson," said Lavinia.

"Who's Bobby Gibson?" asked Chuck, refilling his coffee cup.

"A boy who lived across the street one summer," replied Lavinia.

"I remember him. He was a real nerd. Skinny little kid. Couldn't catch a baseball if it dropped in his lap, but we needed him to make up a team. We stuck him in the outfield." Chuck went back to the football game.

Peggy and Lavinia collapsed in giggles.

"Beauty is in the eye of the beholder," said Peggy, setting off a fresh round of giggles. Then she added, "But we've got more serious problems than puppy love to think about."

"Like what?" asked Lavinia.

"Like who sent the letters to Papa Luigi for starters," said Peggy.

"Give me that magnifying glass," said Lavinia. She studied the envelope fragment.

"What are you looking at?"

"I'm trying to read the postmark. See if you can make it out." Lavinia handed the envelope and magnifying glass to Peggy.

Peggy studied the envelope, moving the magnifying glass up and down to get a better view. Finally she put the magnifying glass down and rubbed her eyes. "I can't read it, it's too fuzzy. It's all dots."

"Where do we go from here?" asked Lavinia.

"I'm too tired to think any more. We'll start fresh in the morning."

Chapter 23

The next morning Peggy was standing in her kitchen wearing her comfortable, but well-worn, terry-cloth robe making waffles for Sunday breakfast when the front doorbell rang. Peggy glanced at the clock. It wasn't even eight. Who could it be at such an early hour?

"I'll get it," said Nicky. "Mom, keep Charlie away from my waffles."

Nicky returned a minute later.

"It's for you, Mom. There's a policeman at the door."

"Is it Henry Cartwright?"

Nicky shook his head before popping a forkful of waffle in his mouth.

Peggy padded to the door, Pie and Buster at her heels.

A uniformed police officer stood outside Peggy's front door. "I'm looking for Mayor Turner," he said. "Is he at home?"

"I'm Mayor Turner," Peggy replied, a smile tugging at her lips.

"My mistake, ma'am, and my apologies."

"For what?" said Peggy. "It's a thankless job, but no one else wants to do it so I keep getting reelected." She wrapped her arms around herself. "It's freezing this morning, won't you come in? What can I do for you?"

"The county said you needed help. So I guess the question is, what can I do for you?"

"Would you like a cup of coffee?"

"That would be nice." He followed Peggy into the kitchen.

Peggy opened the back door and shooed the animals outside. Then she turned back to the officer. "I'm sorry, I didn't catch your name."

"Rob Gibson."

Peggy did a double take.

"Is something wrong, ma'am?"

"Do I know you?" asked Peggy. "Have we met before?"

"I didn't think you'd remember," he said with a smile. "I was only here for a summer, and it was a very long time ago."

Peggy put a hand on Nicky's shoulder. "This is my son Nicky." She turned to Rob. "Bobby, er, ah, Rob, do you remember Lavinia?"

"She lived next door. You two were inseparable."

"She still lives next door. This is her son Charlie."

The boys looked up from their waffles, mumbled hello, and continued eating.

"Have some coffee, I'll be right back." Peggy fled upstairs to get dressed. She spotted Lavinia in her kitchen and called her on the phone.

"Lovey, get over here pronto. You'll never guess in a million years who's sitting in my kitchen."

Peggy threw on a pair of jeans and a sweatshirt, ran a brush through her hair and was back downstairs as Chuck and Lavinia came in through the kitchen door.

"Rob, you remember Lavinia. This is her husband, Chuck Cooper. This is Rob Gibson."

"*Bobby* Gibson?" said Lavinia. "I don't believe it."

"You sure have changed," said Chuck, holding out his hand. "What brings you to Cobb's Landing?"

"I'm with the county police force," said Rob, shaking hands with Chuck. "I've been assigned here on temporary duty."

Peggy started a fresh pot of coffee and began frying bacon. "There's juice on the table. Here are some glasses. Who wants waffles? Boys, if you're finished, you can clear your plates." Peggy arranged waffles on a cookie sheet and popped them in the oven.

The boys went outside to play.

"Nice looking boys," commented Rob. "How old are they? Ten? Eleven? I have a daughter that age."

"Really," said Lavinia. "Do you have any other children?"

"Just Emily."

"Bring her over some day to meet Nicky and Charlie," said Peggy. "Where do you live?"

"I moved to Grover's Corners a month ago, but Emily lives with her mother in Boston."

"*Oh,*" said Lavinia.

"Lovey," said Peggy, "how about putting some plates and silverware on the table. The bacon and waffles are almost ready."

"How long have you been a cop?" asked Chuck.

"Five years," replied Rob. "I played ball for a while after college until my knee went out."

"Who'd you play for?"

"Boston Red Sox."

Chuck let out a low whistle. "What did you play?"

"Outfield."

Chuck choked on his coffee. Lavinia pounded him on the back until his coughing subsided.

"Nicky and Charlie are baseball nuts," Peggy said quickly, before Chuck put his other foot in his mouth.

"It's a great game," said Rob.

"You follow football?" asked Chuck. "There's a game on this afternoon, if you want to come over and watch it."

"Thanks, I'd like that. But I think I'd better tend to some police business before kick-off. What do you do now?"

"I teach shop at the local high school."

"Don't be so modest, honey," said Lavinia. "Chuck also designs and makes reproduction furniture."

"That's quite a talent," said Rob. "I remember you from that summer. You hung around the baseball field with a couple of other kids. Let's see, one was named Tom, and the other was . . . Stu. Have I got it right?"

"Tom was my late husband," said Peggy.

"Tom's Tools and Hardware over on Main Street?"

"I run it now," said Peggy.

"Stu McIntyre was our police chief," said Lavinia.

"Was? What happened to him?"

"He's on an extended leave of absence," said Peggy, putting platters of waffles and bacon on the table. "Henry Cartwright is his replacement. Why don't we have breakfast while it's hot? Help yourself, everybody."

When the waffles and bacon were gone and second cups of coffee poured, Peggy asked Rob, "What became of your grandparents?"

"They moved to Florida the summer after I stayed here. My grandmother suffered from arthritis. A warm climate was supposed to be better for her."

"Was it?"

"It helped. They were happy in Florida. No snow to shovel."

Everyone smiled. Rob looked at Peggy and Lavinia. "And what about your parents? They were very kind to me that summer." He turned to Peggy, "Your mother always made extra cookies for me."

"My parents were killed in a car accident a month after Tom and I were married," said Peggy.

"I'm sorry," said Rob. "Well, if everyone will excuse us, Peggy and I have police business to discuss."

"I can take a hint," said Lavinia.

163

"Thanks for breakfast, PJ, and for keeping Charlie here last night."

"Offer's still good for the game this afternoon," said Chuck, as he and Lavinia went out the kitchen door.

"Thanks, I'll take you up on it," said Rob.

Peggy cleared the table. "More coffee?"

Rob shook his head. He pulled a notebook and pen from his pocket. "Bring me up to date."

Peggy threw up her hands. "Where to begin?"

Rob smiled. "How about at the beginning?"

"But it's hard to tell exactly when things begin, isn't it?"

"Let's accept the fact that every crime on earth had its origin in the Garden of Eden and proceed from there, shall we?"

"I see your point." Peggy laughed. "Skipping forward a few thousand years, I think this started about ten days ago. On a Thursday. It was very warm that day. Indian summer."

Rob nodded and began writing.

Peggy continued, "The school children were going on a field trip to Alsop's woods to collect leaves for their botany scrapbooks. Charlie and Nicky were expelled that day for shooting spitballs in English class and missed the trip."

Rob covered his grin with a slight cough and waited for Peggy to collect her thoughts.

"I went to Alsop's bakery to buy lunch for the boys — I'd put them to work raking leaves on the town square — and Maria came running in to say there was a body in the woods."

"Maria?"

"Maria Alsop. She's a classmate of Nicky and Charlie. Her parents, Gina and Lew, own the bakery. It's her grandfather, Papa Luigi, who was missing."

"And was there a body?"

"Yes and no."

"I don't follow you."

"There was a body, dressed in a Count Dracula costume, but it turned out to be only Buddy."

"Buddy?"

"Buddy is the skeleton in the high school science department. It was apparently a Halloween prank."

"I see," said Rob. "Then what happened?"

"The next morning Buddy showed up again. This time he was in the horse trough."

"Still dressed as Count Dracula?"

Peggy nodded. "When I took Buddy back to the science room, Milt Flask, the science teacher, swore to me he'd locked the room the night before, and he had the only key." Peggy reached for the Citizen's Bank calendar that hung on her kitchen wall. "So much has happened in such a short time, I want to get the sequence right." She looked at the calendar. "Right. That was Friday morning. A week before Halloween. Saturday, Lavinia and I took the kids to the mall to buy their Halloween costumes. I went grocery shopping at the mall, and when I went to put the groceries in the trunk of my car, the costume was gone."

"Which costume?"

"The Count Dracula costume. The second one. The first one I used to decorate my store window."

"Someone broke into your car?"

"Either that or I forgot to lock the trunk. But I don't think so, I always lock my trunk."

"Did you report it?"

Peggy shook her head. "Henry Cartwright and I weren't getting along very well. He thought I was trying to usurp his position by not calling him when Buddy was found in the horse trough."

"Was that the last of Buddy?"

"No. He showed up one more time." Peggy looked at the calendar. "Thursday morning, the day before Halloween. He was on the waterwheel at the former button factory. But this time the perp was caught in the act."

"Who was it?"

"Roger Cartwright."

"The chief's kid?"

Peggy nodded. "Max decided not to press charges and released Roger to the custody of his parents."

"I'll want to interview Roger Cartwright sometime today."

Peggy stared at Rob, then slapped her forehead with the heel of her hand. "Didn't anyone tell you? Roger is dead. I found his body next to Papa Luigi."

"Wait a minute. I'm confused. Let's back up a bit. First, who is Max?"

Peggy rolled her eyes. "Max is an entity unto himself. If we start talking about Max we'll be sitting here until Christmas. Once you meet Max, you'll see what I mean. But if it weren't for Max, Cobb's Landing would be a ghost town. Colonial Village was his idea. Max owns the Citizen's Bank and the former button factory. It's now an inn."

"I'm staying there," said Rob. "Nice rooms." He scanned his notes. "So far, we have a skeleton appearing three times in three different places, a Halloween costume missing from your car trunk, and Roger Cartwright caught in the act of putting the skeleton on the waterwheel at the inn. But you said Roger is dead. Tell me again. Who is Papa Luigi?"

"The man who was missing."

Rob flipped back a page. "Right. Tell me about that."

"Gina called me Thursday morning to say Papa Luigi was missing."

"How long had he been gone?"

"Gina wasn't sure. She last saw him Wednesday evening when she took him his dinner, and he was gone Thursday morning when she returned with breakfast."

"He lives where?"

"In Alsop's woods. Papa Luigi owns all the land. He built a house there when his son Lew married Gina. He gave them his house in Cobb's Landing as a wedding present."

"Lewie Alsop? I remember him," said Rob. "He was a nice kid and a great pitcher. It'll be good to see him again."

"Lew is in Iraq with the National Guard."

Rob exhaled slowly. "That's tough. When is his tour over?"

"Gina hopes he'll be home by Christmas."

"One way or another."

Peggy stared at Rob. "Don't say that. Don't even think it. Lew is a good man."

"They all are, Peggy. My brother was a good man."

Peggy reached over to touch Rob's arm. "I'm so sorry. When did it happen?"

"A year ago. He was one of the first casualties. My parents live in Manchester. The whole town turned out for Mike's funeral."

"Was he older or younger?"

"He was born right before I came here for summer vacation. There were complications. My mother needed prolonged bed rest, so I was sent to stay with my grandparents for the summer."

The phone rang. Peggy glanced at the clock. Nine-fifteen. She answered, then held out the receiver to Rob. "It's for you."

Peggy busied herself with the breakfast dishes while Rob carried on his conversation.

"That was the county. They were going to send someone else here to work with me, but they're still short-staffed. I'd better

169

get over to the Cartwrights'. I'm supposed to touch base with Henry."

"I'll drive you there," said Peggy. "First I need to let Nicky know where I'm going."

"After we stop at the Cartrights', I want to see where you found Roger's body."

"There isn't much to see," said Peggy. "I found him in a small cave in the woods."

Rob whistled. "This case gets more complicated every minute."

The midmorning air was crisp and clear. While Peggy put on a jacket and picked up her rubber boots, Rob stood gazing at the house that had once belonged to his grandparents.

"Do you want to go over there?" asked Peggy. "The present owners are a retired couple, the Murphys. They're only here a few months a year."

"What happens to the house when they're away?"

"They sometimes rent it to schoolteachers. This year it's vacant. Lavinia and I are keeping an eye on it for them."

"I just want to walk around the outside. It won't take long."

Peggy and Rob walked across Maple Street to a gray Cape Cod–style house with black trim. Parallel tracks of concrete with a strip of grass between them led to a single-car garage on the rear of the lot. Peggy stood on the sidewalk while Rob walked up the drive and around the house.

He returned less than a minute later. "House is still in good shape. It looks smaller than I remember."

Peggy smiled. "I sometimes feel that way about my own house. Especially when I look at the years of accumulation."

"Let's go to the Cartwrights' and get it over with."

Peggy tossed her rubber boots in the backseat of her car. For the third time in less than twenty-four hours, Peggy went to the Cartwright house and Carole Ann Cartwright answered the door.

This time Rob did the talking. "Mrs. Cartwright, I'm Robert Gibson from the county police. I'm sorry to trouble you, but I need to confer with your husband. Is he at home?"

Ignoring Peggy completely, Carole Ann replied, "Chief Cartwright has gone to see the medical examiner. He should be back shortly. Won't you come in?"

Peggy followed in Rob's footsteps as silently as a shadow.

"Mrs. Cartwright," said Rob, "I'm truly sorry for your loss. This can't be an easy time for you."

Carole Ann looked at Rob as if he were speaking in tongues. "Save your sympathy for the chief. Roger wasn't my son."

Chapter 24

Rob recovered quickly. Peggy was left standing with her mouth open.

"Roger was Chief Cartwright's son," said Carole Ann. "Roger's mother died ten years ago, when Roger was seven."

"You raised the boy?" asked Rob.

Carole Ann shook her head. "The chief was divorced from his second wife when we got married two years ago. Roger lived with us for the past year. Before that, he was away at school."

That's not the way I heard it, Peggy thought to herself. She kept her mouth clamped shut.

"While I wait for Chief Cartwright, would you mind if I looked in Roger's room?"

Carole Ann hesitated.

"I can get a search warrant," said Rob.

"That won't be necessary," said Carole Ann. She led the way upstairs to the second floor.

The door to Roger's room was secured

with a hasp and combination padlock like the ones kids use on their school and gym lockers. A sign on the door read KEEP OUT.

"Roger was very private," said Carole Ann, spinning the dial on the padlock. "But I once found the combination in the pocket of his jeans." The lock popped open.

The bedroom walls had been painted black, making the room as dark as a cave. Carole Ann pulled back the drapes, flooding the room with sunlight. The room was teenage messy. Unmade bed, clothes strewn everywhere, heavy-metal posters taped to the wall. A TV, DVD player, expensive stereo system, and enough DVDs and CDs to stock a small store filled several shelves. On the desk were a late-model laptop computer, scanner, and color printer.

Rob opened the closet door. Inside were jeans, sweaters, and a worn, black leather jacket. The oak plank closet floor was littered with assorted pairs of black leather boots.

"Did Roger have an after-school or weekend job?" asked Rob.

Carole Ann shook her head.

"Then he must have had a very generous allowance," said Rob.

"I wouldn't know," said Carole Ann. "The chief handles all the household finances."

Rob sat at the desk and began opening drawers. From one drawer he pulled out a plastic bag. "What have we here?" Peggy leaned forward to look as Rob spilled the contents onto the desktop. He pulled one object from the pile of trinkets and held it in the air. "Where did this come from?"

Peggy spoke for the first time since entering the Cartwright house. "That's my charm bracelet!"

"Are you sure?" asked Rob.

"As sure as I'm standing here," said Peggy, reaching for the bracelet.

Rob shook his head. "I'm afraid we'll have to hold onto this for now. When did you lose it?"

"I noticed it was missing a week ago," said Peggy. "Lavinia can back me up. She was at my house when I was looking for it. Tom gave me that bracelet and all the charms on it. I can name them from memory." Peggy closed her eyes. "Football, wishing well, engagement ring, heart engraved with our initials, wedding cake, teddy bear, hammer, and a small round disk with Nicky's name and birth date."

Carole Ann took the bracelet from Rob and handed it to Peggy. "Take your bracelet. Roger had a history of bullying little children for their lunch money, but I didn't know he'd added petty theft to his list of dubious achievements. You can't know how sorry I am."

Peggy thanked Carole Ann and slipped the bracelet into her purse.

Carole Ann looked at the pile of trinkets on the desk. "See if you can find the rightful owners and return those, too. I don't want any part of them. The truth is, I don't want to be part of any of this." She turned on her heel and left the room. She returned a minute later and put a key in Peggy's hand. "Lock up when you leave. You can give the key to the chief."

Peggy heard Carole Ann go down the steps, then leave the house. The front door slammed shut. Carole Ann got into her car and drove away.

"Now what do we do?" Peggy asked Rob.

Rob was busy looking through another desk drawer. He thumbed through the contents of a file folder, then handed it to Peggy. "What do you make of this?"

Peggy sat on the edge of the bed and looked through the papers in the file.

"These are the same letters that Papa Luigi received."

"What letters?"

"Let's get out of here, and I'll tell you." Peggy shuddered as she looked around the room. "This room is giving me the creeps."

Rob took the file folder and laptop computer.

As they were descending the stairs, the front door flew open. Henry Cartwright stood in the doorway, his hand resting on his gun. He glared at Rob. "Who in the hell are you, and what are you doing in my house?"

Chapter 25

Leaving the Cartwrights', Peggy drove down Main Street toward the Rock River.

"Is today your first time back in Cobb's Landing?" asked Peggy. She needed a diversion from the scene with Henry that was still echoing in her head.

Rob nodded. "I never had a reason to come back until now. But it feels like I've never been away. This town has an ageless quality. It wears well."

"You should have seen it a year ago. It wasn't so pretty then. You came back at the right time."

Peggy parked at the end of Main Street and they walked down to the Rock River. Peggy looked at Rob's feet. "You might want to put on some boots. The going gets a little rough."

Peggy waited outside the inn while Rob went inside to change. When he returned, they continued their walk.

"This is where we had the pumpkin float Friday night."

"Pumpkin float?"

Peggy explained about the Halloween festivities while they walked along the river bank. They reached the rocks. Only fragments of pumpkins remained, the river was once again following its natural course.

"I came back here yesterday morning to find Maria's pumpkin," said Peggy. "The pileup of pumpkins on the rocks created a dam, with the runoff heading in this direction." Peggy put on her gloves and headed right, pushing her way through briars, brambles, and branches, counting her steps under her breath. Suddenly she stopped. "It's gone."

Rob looked around the woods. "What's gone?"

"Maria's pumpkin. I left it at the base of this tree to mark the spot."

"Are you sure this is the right place?"

"Positive." She pointed to the bushes a few yards away. "The cave is over there."

Rob reached into his jacket pocket and pulled out an aluminum object about the size of a deck of cards. A black plastic rectangle protruded from the top. He opened the case and pushed a button.

Peggy looked at the object in his hands. "What's that?"

"A handheld computer. It's an iPAQ."

He pulled the stylus out of its holder and tapped the screen a few times, then pointed to the black rectangle. "This is a GPS."

"A what?"

"Global positioning system. Wait a sec, and I'll show you." He held the unit aloft and kept watching the screen. "Okay, we've got a reading." He tapped the screen a few more times, then handed the iPAQ to Peggy. "Take a look. It's a map of the area. The red *X* shows where we are right now."

Peggy held the unit in her hands as carefully as a newly laid egg. "Wow. Nicky would love this." She handed it back to Rob.

Rob pulled the GPS out of the iPAQ and inserted another device. He tapped the screen again and held the iPAQ facing Peggy. "Say 'cheese.' "

"What's that?"

"A digital camera." He took several pictures of the area. "Now show me the cave."

Peggy pushed through the bushes concealing the cave entrance. "Here we are."

Rob looked around. He took a few more pictures. "Tell me where the bodies were."

Peggy stood with her back to the cave entrance. "Papa Luigi was lying on the left. His feet were tied. Next to him was a gun."

She pointed to the right. "There was the figure dressed as Count Dracula. At first I thought it was Buddy. Then we discovered it was Roger Cartwright. He'd been shot in the chest."

Rob reached for Peggy's hand. "Let's get out of here. I've seen everything I need to for now."

They made their way back to the Rock River, and then to the inn. "Is there any place we can get a bite to eat?" asked Rob. "The restaurant at the inn is closed until dinner."

Peggy shook her head. "It's Sunday. Clemmie's Cafe is closed today."

"Clemmie's is still around? My grandpa and I used to head over there for a hamburger on Saturday afternoons when grandma was busy digging in her garden."

"It's under new management, but it's still the same old Clemmie's. Same decor, same menu."

" 'If it ain't fried, it ain't food' should have been their motto. They had the best French fries I've ever tasted."

"If soup and a sandwich is okay with you, you're welcome to lunch at my house," said Peggy. "I need to get home to check on Nicky."

"I want to look at the contents of

Roger's computer," said Rob, "and I want to hear about the letters that were sent to Papa Luigi."

Lavinia poked her head out her front door as Peggy was getting out of her car. "Nicky's at our house, PJ. We're just about to have chili and cornbread for lunch. C'mon over."

Peggy pulled her charm bracelet from her purse and held it up in the air. "Lovey! I found my charm bracelet!"

"Where was it?"

"Roger Cartwright stole it." Peggy crossed over to Lavinia's front yard as Nicky and Charlie approached at a run from the Cooper's backyard. Nicky stopped short when he saw the bracelet in his mother's hand.

Chapter 26

"Nicky, how about another bowl of chili?" asked Lavinia.

"I don't think so," said Nicky.

"No, thank you," prompted Peggy.

"No, thank you," said Nicky.

"You love my chili," said Lavinia. "You always have more than one bowl."

"Are you feeling all right?" asked Peggy.

"Not really," said Nicky.

"Why don't you go home," said Peggy. "I'll look in on you in a little while."

Nicky picked up his jacket and left the Cooper's through the kitchen door. Peggy watched through the window until Nicky was inside his own house.

"He seemed okay this morning, PJ," said Lavinia.

"Could be one of those twenty-four hour things," said Peggy. "Or maybe he's not over his Friday night pig-out. He ate so much Halloween candy when we got home, he made himself sick." Peggy held out her bowl to Lavinia. " 'Please, sir, may

I have some more?' "

Lavinia laughed. "Help yourself, there's plenty. Rob? How about you?"

"Is there any more of that delicious cornbread? It tastes like the corn muffins my grandmother used to make."

"I'm not surprised," said Lavinia. "Your grandmother gave my mother the recipe. It's been a favorite in our family for years."

"It's almost kick-off time," said Chuck. "Keep the chili hot, honey, I'll have another bowl during the half."

"Be right there," said Rob, finishing his buttered corn bread. "Thank you, Lavinia. It was a wonderful lunch."

Peggy and Lavinia sat at the kitchen table savoring their second bowls of chili, while sounds of football were heard in the background.

"Tell me everything," said Lavinia. "I can't believe you went sleuthing without me."

"Lovey, I think the Cartwrights put the *d* in dysfunctional. Did you know that Carole Ann is Henry's third wife?"

Lavinia's eyes popped. "You're kidding."

"According to Carole Ann, Roger's mother — Henry's first wife — died when Roger was seven. I'd love to know what happened to her. Henry was divorced from his second wife when he married Carole Ann two years ago."

"Well, that sort of explains Roger, doesn't it?"

Peggy sighed. "You almost have to feel sorry for that kid. Carole Ann said Roger had been away at school until he came to live with them a year ago."

"Oh, really?" said Lavinia. "That's putting a pretty face on it. Didn't Ian say Roger had been in juvenile detention? In my book, that's called reform school."

"I agree," said Peggy. "Carole Ann also said that Roger had a history of bullying little children for their lunch money, but she wasn't aware he'd graduated to petty theft."

"Whew! What a piece of work. Jesus, PJ, it makes you wonder how we got so lucky with our kids."

Peggy nodded. "I can't imagine it was any picnic growing up with Henry for a father. That man is a real martinet. He was career military before he joined the police force."

"That figures," said Lavinia.

"I think Carole Ann was afraid of him," said Peggy.

"What makes you think so?"

"Just the way she acted around him. Not that I saw them together that often, but she seemed very deferential and also eager for his approval."

"It could also account for why she was such a bitch in the classroom," said Lavinia. "Granted, spitballs are not acceptable behavior — I've already had a stern talk with Charlie about it and warned him what will happen if he ever does it again — but expelling the boys was excessive."

"I'm with you on both counts," said Peggy. "I've had the same talk with Nicky."

"So," said Lavinia, "you went to the Cartwrights' house with Rob. Then what happened?"

"Henry wasn't home. He'd gone to see the medical examiner. Carole Ann grudgingly let us look in Roger's room, after she informed us Roger was not her son."

"That must have come as a surprise," said Lavinia.

"You could have knocked me over with a feather," Peggy replied. "But the real surprise was Roger's room. The kid had it padlocked shut from the outside."

"You're kidding."

"I wish I were. However, Carole Ann knew the combination and let us inside. Can you believe it? The walls were painted black."

"Black?"

Peggy nodded. "Black. With the curtains closed, it was like being in a cave."

"Bad choice of words, PJ."

Peggy grinned. "You haven't heard anything yet. The kid had a king's ransom worth of electronic equipment in that room. State-of-the-art stereo, television, DVD player, and computer."

"Where did he get the money to pay for it?"

"I don't know. But I'll tell you, it was better than anything I have in my house."

"Where was your bracelet?"

"In one of Roger's desk drawers. In a plastic bag with a bunch of trinkets. That's when Carole Ann lost it."

"What do you mean?"

"When I told Rob it was mine, he was planning on holding it for evidence. But after I named all the charms on the bracelet, Carole Ann insisted it be given back to me. Then she marched out of the room, down the stairs, out the front door, got into her car, and drove away."

"Where do you think she went?"

"I don't know, Lovey. But I have a sneaking feeling she won't be back."

"Oh my," said Lavinia.

"Wait until you hear this. Rob found a folder of letters in Roger's desk drawer."

"What kind of letters?"

"The same ones that were sent to Papa Luigi."

"You're kidding. Do you think Roger was being scammed too?"

Peggy shook her head. "I think Roger was scamming Papa Luigi, and Missy was in on it."

"Missy? What's she got to do with it?" asked Lavinia.

"Don't you remember that exchange we overheard at Papa Luigi's house last weekend? With Missy?"

"Right. I'd forgotten. What did she say to Papa Luigi? Something about signing papers and a payoff."

"We need to find out about that, Lovey. I told you when Missy first came back that she was up to no good. I never trusted her."

"What happened after Carole Ann left?"

"It was creepy being in that room with no one else in the house. Rob took the folder of letters and Roger's laptop computer. We were heading down the stairs when the front door flew open. There stood Henry with his hand on his gun."

"Oh, my God."

"Henry looked at Rob and said 'Who are you and what are you doing in my house?'

It's a good thing Rob was in uniform. Henry looked like he had an itchy trigger finger."

"Were you scared?"

"Not really, I find Henry more irritating than intimidating."

Lavinia giggled. "Then what?"

"Rob explained who he was and what he was doing there and that Carole Ann had let us in."

"What did Henry say?"

"He wanted to know where Carole Ann was. We had no idea. Rob explained to Henry that it was a conflict of interest for him to be investigating the death of his son and that Rob would be taking over temporarily — on orders from the county — until the case was solved."

"How did Henry react?"

"How do you think? But Henry acted like he understood why. I feel a lot better having Rob here. But there's one thing that scares me."

"What's that, PJ?"

"I'm afraid Papa Luigi is going to be arrested for Roger's murder."

Chapter 27

During halftime, Peggy went home to check on Nicky. She found him in his room, lying on his bed fully clothed, huddled under his patchwork quilt. She put her hand on Nicky's forehead. He felt slightly moist and feverish.

"Nicky, tell me what's wrong. Do you want me to call the doctor?"

Nicky shook his head. In a small voice he said, "Roger Cartwright didn't steal your bracelet. I did."

Peggy sat on the edge of Nicky's bed, feeling like someone had let all the air out of her. "Why, Nicky?"

"I gave it to Maria. I wanted her to like me better than Charlie."

"Oh, Nicky." Peggy shook her head slowly, completely at a loss for words. After a long moment, she looked at her son. "Don't move. I'll be right back."

Peggy went to her room and made a quick phone call. Then she went back to Nicky's room. "Go wash your face. Then we're going over to Maria's house."

Nicky turned pale. "Do we have to?"

"Yes, Nicky. We have to."

"But Maria will hate me."

Peggy reached for her son's hands and squeezed them. "Sit down, Nicky. First we'll talk."

Nicky sat on his bed, too ashamed to look at his mother.

Peggy cupped her hand under her son's chin, forcing him to look her in the eye. "You know what you did was wrong, don't you?"

Nicky nodded.

"Taking anything that doesn't belong to you is wrong. Taking an apple from a tree that's not yours is as wrong as stealing a bracelet. Do you understand that?"

"Yes, Mom. I understand. I'm really sorry."

"Nicky, you and I are a family. And families have to trust each other. Because without trust, then we're two strangers living under the same roof. How would you feel if I came into your room while you were at school and took your stamp collection or stole money out of your piggy bank and later lied about it?"

Tears rolled down Nicky's cheeks.

Peggy held her son and stroked his hair. "You really like Maria, don't you?"

Nicky nodded, wiping away the tears with the back of his hand.

"Nicky, liking someone and having them like you back depends on what you are as a person, not what you give them. Do you understand that?"

Nicky thought for a moment. "My daddy gave you that bracelet, and you liked him."

"But that wasn't why I liked him. I liked your father for a long time before he gave me the bracelet."

"How long?"

"Years, Nicky. Your father and I grew up together here in Cobb's Landing. He gave me the bracelet when we graduated from high school. It's our life together. Here. I'll show you." Peggy pulled the gold bracelet from her pocket. "When he gave me the bracelet, only the football was on it. He won that football our senior year in high school and worked weekends to earn the money to buy the bracelet." Her fingers moved to the wishing well. "He bought this charm when I graduated from junior college, and the engagement ring because he couldn't afford to buy me a real one, the heart was for my birthday before we got married, the wedding cake was his present to me when we got married. The teddy bear was for you. The hammer is for the hardware store and this . . ." Peggy fondled the disk with Nicky's name and birth date, "he gave to me the day after you were born. Every charm has a special meaning."

"If it's so special, why don't you wear it?"

Peggy slipped the bracelet back in her pocket. "I stopped wearing it after your father died because looking at it made me miss him."

"Do you still miss him?"

"Every day. But I have you, Nicky. And you're as special to me as he was."

"Will you ever get married again?"

"When I meet someone I like as much as I liked your father. Someone who's honest, someone I can trust. Someone who doesn't lie to me. Someone who makes me laugh. Someone who is first a friend. That's what makes someone special. Tell me, why do you like Maria?"

"Because she's pretty, and she's smart." Nicky blushed. "She smells like flowers."

"Why do you think Maria likes you?"

"I don't know." Nicky shook his head. "She laughs at Charlie when he wiggles his ears in English class."

"Is that what happened the day you and Charlie were expelled?"

"Yeah. It was really boring, and I looked at Maria, but she was looking at Charlie and laughing when he wiggled his ears. So I hit him with a spitball, and Maria smiled at me. Then Charlie hit me back and everyone laughed and Mrs. Cartwright got mad and sent us to the principal's office."

Peggy sighed. She put her arm around her son and hugged him. "Nicky, Maria likes you because you're smart, because you're a good person. Not because you hit Charlie with a spitball or give her presents. Those are the wrong reasons to like someone and that kind of liking doesn't last. Is that why Maria gave you the stamps? Because you gave her the bracelet?"

Nicky nodded. "Do I have to give the stamps back? I know Ian said they're not worth anything. But Maria gave them to me."

"That's up to Maria's mother."

"Mom, do we really have to go over there?"

"Yes, Nicky, we do."

"I'm really sorry about taking your bracelet."

"I know you are." Peggy hugged her son. "I love you, Nicky."

"I love you, too, Mom."

"Wash your face, then we'll go."

Nicky was quiet on the drive to Maria's house. Gina greeted them at the door. "Hi, Peggy. Hello, Nicky. Maria and I were just getting ready to go to the hospital to visit Papa Luigi."

"This won't take long, Gina."

The two mothers and their children sat in Gina's living room. Peggy felt like she was walking on tiptoe through a minefield. I hope I've done the right thing by coming here, she thought, taking the bracelet out of her pocket. She showed it to Maria. "Maria, is this the bracelet that Nicky gave you?"

Maria's eyes grew big. "Yes."

"Maria, you didn't tell me," said Gina. "The bracelet is very pretty, but far too extravagant for a girl your age."

"It's really mine, Gina. But that's not the reason we're here." Peggy turned to Maria. "Maria, this bracelet was found today at Roger Cartwright's house. Do you know how it got there?"

Maria nodded, not looking at her mother.

What a dunce I am, thought Peggy. Why didn't I figure it out earlier? Peggy said aloud, "Maria, tell me how Roger got the bracelet."

"I gave it to him," Maria said matter-of-factly.

"Why, Maria?" asked Gina.

195

"Because . . ." Maria's voice faltered.

"Maria," said Peggy. "Was Roger Cartwright the wolf?"

Maria nodded, emitting a soft sigh of relief that it was finally out in the open.

"Peggy, what's this all about?" Gina looked at her daughter. "What wolf?"

"Gina, this afternoon Carole Ann Cartwright told me that Roger had a history of bullying younger children." Peggy turned again to Maria. "Was Roger the one in the woods when you went to take dinner to Papa Luigi?"

Maria nodded.

"And also at the mall the day we went shopping for the Halloween costumes?"

Maria nodded again.

"Maria, why didn't you tell me?" asked Gina.

"Gina," said Peggy, "you've had a lot on your mind with Lew away. Maria thought she was doing the right thing by not adding to your burdens."

"Maria," said Gina. "I'm your mother. I'm supposed to be the grownup, the one who does the worrying for you, the one who takes care of you." Gina reached for her daughter and held her tight.

Peggy felt tears tickling her eyes and blinked them away.

Maria hugged her mother. "Don't worry, Mama, everything's okay. Grandpa Luigi fixed it."

"What do you mean, Maria?" asked Peggy.

"I told grandpa about the wolf. He promised me he'd fix it so the wolf never bothered me again."

Chapter 28

Peggy was silent on the drive home.

"Are you still mad at me?" asked Nicky.

"No, Nicky, I'm not angry. I'm thinking."

Nicky knew better than to interrupt. He also knew he was still in deep doo-doo. When they got home, he went straight to his room and started in on his homework.

Peggy sat at her kitchen table watching the late afternoon sun sink behind the pine trees in her backyard. It was the light of approaching winter: pale, lacking the golden aura of spring and summer. Soon there would be snow on the pines. Peggy thought about Roger Cartwright. How does a child go bad? Is there really such a thing as a bad seed? The old debate over heredity versus environment. Having his mother die when he was seven must have been a contributing factor. That coupled with being a military brat and having a disciplinarian like Henry for a father. Who knows what Henry's second wife was like?

It was obvious to Peggy that Carole Ann had no love for her stepson.

Peggy was more upset about the theft of her bracelet than she let on to Nicky. Upset because Nicky had taken something that didn't belong to him and then lied about it the first time she asked him. If she hadn't found the bracelet in Roger's desk drawer, she wondered if Nicky would ever have told her the truth. What really troubled Peggy was wondering if Nicky was headed down the same path as Roger Cartwright. Short of riding Nicky's butt 24/7, what could a parent do? Peggy prayed that this was a onetime incident and Nicky would grow out of it as he got through his first brush with puppy love. Peggy put her head in her hands and sighed.

"PJ, are you all right?"

"Lovey! I didn't hear you come in. Have you been taking lessons from Max?"

Peggy noticed that Lavinia was dressed in her nurse's uniform. "I thought you were off this weekend?"

"I was, until a few minutes ago. One of the weekend nurses called in sick. I've got to sub. I really came over to tell you that Chuck and Charlie are having sloppy joes made with the leftover chili. There's plenty to go around. Why don't you and Nicky head over to our house for supper? Rob's still there watching football with Chuck."

"Thanks, Lovey. That sounds good."

Lavinia reached down and hugged her friend. "Whatever's bothering you, I want to know about. But later. Okay?" Lavinia paused in the kitchen doorway to blow a kiss to Peggy, then sprinted out Peggy's front door.

Peggy went upstairs. "C'mon, Nicky. We're going over to the Coopers' for sloppy joes."

"Are you going to tell what I did? Will Mr. Gibson put me in jail?"

"Not this time, Nicky." Peggy smiled. "I'll let you off for good behavior. But don't let it happen again."

"I won't, Mom. I promise." Nicky crossed his heart.

I've got to believe in my son, thought Peggy.

After supper at the Coopers', Rob Gibson walked over to the Turner house with Peggy and Nick.

Nicky went into the living room to watch television while Peggy and Rob explored the contents of Roger Cartwright's laptop computer. Rob tapped the keys while Peggy looked over his shoulder.

He explored the directory of Roger's

hard drive, then clicked on a file. A few seconds later a graphic appeared on the screen.

"The stamps!" said Peggy. "Those are the stamps that were on the letters Papa Luigi received. Wait, I'll show you." Peggy went to get the file of letters she'd borrowed from Gina. "Nicky! Get your stamp collection and bring it to the kitchen."

They compared the stamps on the screen with the stamps on the envelopes Papa Luigi received and the ones Maria had given Nicky. Even the postmarks matched.

Rob sat scratching his head. "I agree we've got a match. But the question is, how did these letters get to Luigi Alsop?"

"Through the mail?" asked Nicky.

Rob shook his head. "Not very likely. You see, Nicky, sending letters like this is a crime in Nigeria. There it's called a four-one-nine fraud because it's named for the section in the Nigerian penal code that makes it illegal for Nigerians to participate in the fraud or to possess any documents used in the scam. It's also illegal to use counterfeit stamps like these . . ." Rob pointed to the computer screen. "Mail bearing counterfeit stamps is usually destroyed before it leaves Nigeria. If a letter with counterfeit postage gets out of Nigeria, then the United States postal inspectors seize the letters when they arrive in this country."

"Why don't they use real stamps?" asked Nicky.

"Too expensive," said Rob. "The people who send letters like this are trying to get something for nothing. Real stamps cost money."

"Why not use a postage meter mark?" asked Peggy. "That would be a lot easier to fake and harder to detect."

Rob shook his head. "Any letter bearing a Nigerian postage meter impression is spotted as a fraud immediately."

"How come?" asked Nicky.

Rob smiled. "Because there are no postage meters in Nigeria."

"Oh."

Rob went back to the hard-drive directory and tapped on another file. A word processing document appeared on the screen. "Well, well, what do we have here?"

Peggy flipped through the file of letters. "It's the first letter Papa Luigi received." She held the letter next to the laptop screen. The contents were identical, down to the commas.

Half an hour later they had matched

every letter to Papa Luigi with files on Roger Cartwright's laptop.

"I'm still puzzled as to how these letters got to Mr. Alsop," said Rob. "I could see one letter slipping past the postal inspectors, but not half a dozen. That doesn't make sense."

Peggy thought for a minute. "These letters were never mailed. Papa Luigi has a mailbox at the end of his driveway. All Roger had to do was go over there and put a letter in the box with the other mail." Peggy put her hand up to her mouth. "Oh, my God. Maria."

"Gina and Lew's daughter? Mr. Alsop's granddaughter? What about her?"

"Maria saw Roger in the woods. He must have been going to or from the mailbox at the time. Maria told me a week ago that she was being bothered by a wolf in the woods and earlier this afternoon she admitted that Roger was the wolf. She also said . . ."

"Said what, Peggy?"

"I shouldn't tell you this. You might get the wrong impression."

"Tell him, Mom," said Nicky. "You have to tell the truth."

Peggy put her arm around her son. "Maria said that she told her grandfather

203

about the wolf in the woods. He promised Maria he'd fix it so the wolf never bothered her again."

"This doesn't look good for Mr. Alsop," said Rob.

"I know," said Peggy. "I know."

The phone rang. Peggy answered it. "We'll be right there." She turned to Rob. "That was Lavinia, calling from the hospital. Papa Luigi has just regained consciousness."

Chapter 29

"Five minutes only." There was no mistaking the doctor's authority, or his inclination to boot them out on their backsides if they overstayed their welcome. "Mr. Alsop has regained consciousness, but he is still in critical condition. I'll permit only two visitors." He turned to Rob. "Who are you?"

Rob flashed his badge. "Robert Gibson of the county police."

"You'll have to wait outside. My patient is in no condition to talk to the police tonight." He turned to Gina. "I'm sorry, no children allowed. Your daughter will have to wait in the lounge."

Peggy and Gina entered the hospital room where Lavinia was on duty at Papa Luigi's bedside. Peggy hung back with Lavinia, while Gina sat on the edge of her father-in-law's bed and took his hand in hers.

Never a man who would be described as portly, Papa Luigi appeared paler and more gaunt than usual. He was sitting up in bed, propped by a pile of pillows. The usual assortment of tubes attached to pouches pumped medication and fluids into his arms — arms which had been muscled from years of kneading bread and rolling out dough and were now slack and riddled with blue veins — while state-of-the-art machines silently recorded all his vital signs.

Lavinia whispered to Peggy, "I've already talked to Papa Luigi. He swears he didn't kill Roger Cartwright, and I believe him."

Gina and Papa Luigi conversed softly in Italian.

The doctor entered the room. "Time's up. My patient needs his rest. You have to leave now."

Gina kissed her father-in-law's left cheek. She switched to English. "This is from me." Then his right cheek. "And this is from Maria." She squeezed his hand gently. "I'll be back tomorrow."

As Peggy and Gina were leaving the room, Lavinia said, "I'll stay with Papa Luigi until my shift is over."

Peggy and Gina went to the lounge where Maria was sitting with Rob Gibson. "Maria, Papa Luigi is going to be just fine. Let's go home, and you can make a card for him. I'll bring it to him tomorrow."

"Mrs. Alsop, may I have a moment?" asked Rob. "Did your father-in-law say anything?"

Gina looked at Rob. "He said he didn't kill Roger, and I believe him. My father-in-law is a man of his word." Gina took Maria's hand and they left the hospital.

On the way back to Cobb's Landing, Peggy said, "Lavinia talked to Papa Luigi and said the same thing. Papa Luigi didn't kill Roger Cartwright."

"You've got to admit, he had motive," said Rob. "First we have the Nigerian scam letters on Roger's computer, and, even more important, Roger was bullying his granddaughter. Those are two strong motives for murder."

"But we have no proof that Roger actually benefited from those letters," said Peggy.

"You're right, Peggy," said Rob. "Until we find the money — if any money changed hands — we can't prove anything. I know you want to believe Mr. Alsop, but my instincts tell me he's guilty."

Peggy stopped the car at the end of Main Street, a short walk from the former button factory. "Damn your instincts. You may have spent a summer here, but that was a long time ago. You don't know the people in Cobb's Landing the way I do."

Rob got out of the car. Before he could say another word, Peggy spun the wheel and headed home.

The next morning Peggy had poured herself a cup of coffee and was making Nicky's breakfast when there was a tap on the kitchen door.

Lavinia stood there, dressed in her nurse's uniform, a cup of coffee in her hand.

"Lovey, are you just now getting home from the hospital?"

"No, I'm on the way back for my regular shift."

"Have you had any sleep?"

"A few hours. I'll need a couple more cups of this, though, before I'm completely wide awake." Lavinia drained the contents of her cup, then held it out to Peggy for a refill. "I know you have to get Nicky off to school, but I wanted to make sure you were all right."

"Of course I am," said Peggy.

"It didn't look that way yesterday afternoon."

"A little misunderstanding with Nicky. I'm more concerned about Papa Luigi. Tell me what he said."

"As you can imagine, PJ, he wasn't completely coherent. The man spent Lord knows how many days with a pneumonia-induced fever that would fry anyone's brain. But he knew who he was and where he was. When I asked him what happened, he mumbled about setting a wolf trap to protect Maria."

"Roger Cartwright being the wolf. Maria admitted she told her grandfather about the wolf in the woods. Papa Luigi said he would make the wolf go away."

"Oh, PJ, that doesn't sound too good for Papa Luigi, does it?"

"Rob Gibson doesn't think so, too. He thinks Papa Luigi is guilty of murder."

"Papa Luigi swears he didn't kill Roger. He said he waited for Roger to leave for school Thursday morning and forced Roger to the cave in the woods at gunpoint. Once they got there, he was tying Roger's feet with rope so he couldn't get away. The next thing Papa Luigi knew, he woke with his own feet tied, his gun at his side, and Roger was dead. By then the fever was raging and he thinks he passed out. When he woke again, Papa Luigi was in the hospital." Lavinia paused to drink some coffee. "I wonder why Henry and Carole Ann didn't report Roger missing?"

"I think I know," said Peggy. "Because of the deal Henry made with Max the morning Roger was caught putting Buddy on the waterwheel. Max released Roger to Henry's custody, but reserved the right to press full charges if Roger was involved in any more funny stuff. If Max found out Roger was missing, he would have been breathing fire like an angry dragon."

"Makes sense to me why Henry kept mum," said Lavinia.

"Did you ask Papa Luigi about the letters from Nigeria?"

"I didn't get a chance, PJ. I'll do it today if I can."

"Roger sent those letters," said Peggy.

"Roger? Roger Cartwright? Are you sure?"

"Almost positive. The exact same letters were on the hard drive of Roger's laptop computer. And a graphic of the stamps."

"I don't get it," said Lavinia.

"Rob explained all about the Nigerian scam," said Peggy. "Using counterfeit postage is illegal, which is why most of the scam letters are confiscated either in Nigeria or, if they somehow get out of that country, when they arrive at their destinations. Most so-called Nigerian scammers today use e-mail or a fax machine. It's cheaper and faster. No postage involved."

"Papa Luigi didn't have a computer or a fax," said Lavinia.

"Exactly. So the only way those letters could have gotten to Papa Luigi was by hand delivery."

"Roger printed the letters on his computer, pasted on the fake postage, then dropped the letters in Papa Luigi's mailbox?"

"You got it, Lovey. Maria must have seen Roger in the woods when he was delivering one of the letters. Roger began bullying Maria so she'd stay away from her grandfather's house. Maria said she saw Roger at the mall the day we went shopping for Halloween costumes."

"Poor Maria." Lavinia poured more coffee into her cup. "PJ, you read those letters. Why would anyone fall for something like that? It's so obviously a hoax."

"Rob said hundreds of people all over the world fall for it every year. People you think would know better, like well-educated businessmen. Some have actually traveled to Nigeria to collect their money. Fifteen businessmen, including one American, have been killed in Nigeria because of the scams."

Lavinia shook her head. "I still can't believe anyone would fall for it. It's like —

what's it called? A pigeon drop — that you read about in the paper every so often. Where someone finds an envelope full of money and offers to split the proceeds. The victim puts up good-faith money and ends up with an envelope of worthless paper."

"I read a story about a man in Massachusetts, a retired police officer, who tried to sell a boat on the Internet and almost lost ten thousand dollars in a bogus check scam."

"What happened?" asked Lavinia.

"He received a check for more than the asking price of the boat. He was supposed to refund the difference in cash by Western Union. But when he took the check he received to his bank, he found out it was bogus, drawn on a non-existent account in Nigeria."

"That sounds as crazy as buying a lottery ticket, thinking you're going to win the Powerball jackpot," said Lavinia. "Have you ever bought a lottery ticket?"

"I did once," said Peggy, blushing at the memory. "I really thought I was going to strike it rich. But all I ended up with was a worthless piece of paper. It was the same as dropping my ten dollars down a sewer grating. I was really mad at myself for being so foolish. I never bought another lottery ticket after that."

"It just proves if it sounds too good to be true, it probably is," said Lavinia.

"Rob thinks that's one motive Papa Luigi had for doing away with Roger."

"What is?"

"The money. If Papa Luigi paid Roger, that's one more motive for murder."

"But Papa Luigi didn't know it was Roger sending the letters. What did you say to Rob, PJ?"

"I told Rob to stuff it," said Peggy.

"Good for you." Lavinia looked at the kitchen clock. "I've got to get to work. And Nicky's going to be late for school. I'll try to talk to Papa Luigi today. You do believe he's innocent, don't you?"

"Of course I do," replied Peggy. "Foolish, yes, but a murderer? Absolutely not."

"There's only one problem, PJ. How are we going to prove it?"

"I've got an idea about the gun," replied Peggy. "I'll let you know later if it pans out."

Chapter 30

After getting Nicky off to school, Peggy ran upstairs to get dressed for work. She went to her closet, reaching for the colonial costume she'd worn every day since Colonial Village opened. Then she paused, a big grin spread across her face. Hot damn. Tourist season was over. No more colonial costume until next spring. No more long skirt twisting around her ankles like eel-grass, hampering every step she took. No more blouse, no more apron, no more shoes that still gave her feet blisters. And no more dorky hat that looked like a ruffle-edged shower cap. Peggy felt like a kid on the first day of summer vacation.

While Peggy had to admit that Colonial Village had been a financial boon to Cobb's Landing, the costumes were a bit much.

She slipped into her most comfortable jeans, grabbed a favorite pullover sweater and a pair of red suede ankle boots that were as easy on her feet as bedroom slippers. She skipped downstairs, tossed a new rawhide chew bone to Buster, put Pie into the cat carrier, then headed for Tom's Tools.

Peggy flipped on the hardware-store lights, released Pie from the carrier, and filled her water bowl. Pie hopped onto the checkout counter for a leisurely bath, licking her front paw and rubbing it in a circle over her head.

Peggy called the medical examiner. When all she got was his answering machine, she left a message asking him to call her as soon as possible.

To pass the time while she waited for the phone to ring, Peggy decided to take down the Halloween decorations in her storefront window. The pumpkin head she'd carved in Max's likeness was beginning to collapse and soon would be a squishy mess. Peggy grabbed a trash bag and went to work.

"It's a shame to let that fine art go to waste."

"Max! Where on earth have you been?"

"Here and there. I'm in great demand at Halloween. It's my busy season."

"Do tell, Max."

Max smiled enigmatically and refused to elaborate. He gazed wistfully around the checkout counter. "I don't suppose there's any candy corn left?"

"Sorry, Max. I gave away the last package to trick or treaters before the pumpkin float. How about a nice cup of hot apple cider?"

Max made a face like he'd bitten into a sour green apple. "I'd rather quaff battery acid."

"I'm sure that can be arranged," said Peggy. "Coffee? Strong and black? It'll be ready in a minute."

Max beamed. When he was through with his second cup, looking as content as Pie after a saucer of cream, Peggy said, "Max, I need your help."

Max set the coffee cup on the counter, then straightened his red silk bow tie. "Do you need to borrow money?"

"*Max*. We've had this discussion before. Not everything revolves around money."

"In my business it does. Tell me what you need."

"Information."

"That's my stock in trade. 'It's not *who* you know . . . ' "

Peggy and Max finished the sentence together, like a Greek chorus. " '. . . it's *what* you know about them.' "

"Let's get down to business," said Max,

briskly rubbing his hands. "What do you want to know about whom?"

"Papa Luigi."

Max waited for Peggy to elaborate.

"I'm afraid he's being scammed."

Max's eyebrows went up a fraction of an inch.

"After I found Papa Luigi Saturday morning in a cave in the woods next to Roger Cartwright's body . . ."

"That boy will be shoveling coal for all eternity," Max said gleefully.

"What?" Peggy look at Max uncomprehendingly. "Where?"

Max pointed downward, jabbing the air several times with the index finger of his right hand.

"*Oh*," said Peggy, her eyes growing wide.

"You thought he sprouted wings . . ." Max held his crossed wrists chest high, hooked his thumbs and fluttered his fingers to imitate flying wings. "And went . . ." Max pointed skyward with a questioning glance, then shook his head emphatically. "Not a chance. I knew where that boy was headed the minute I laid eyes on him."

Peggy smiled. "Max, sometimes you're a little spooky. You know that?"

Max preened. "I pride myself on it. Keeps everyone on their toes."

"About Papa Luigi . . ."

"What about him?"

Peggy explained about the Nigerian scam letters she'd found and the large cash withdrawals on Papa Luigi's bank statements. She didn't mention her suspicion that Roger was behind the letters.

"You want me to disclose private information about one of my bank customers?" asked Max.

Peggy nodded.

"There are federal banking rules about that," Max said sternly. Then he shrugged and smiled. "But rules are meant to be broken. What will you give me for the information?"

Peggy reached for the red silk bow tie she'd removed from the Halloween figure in her store window and held it high in the air, dangling from her fingertips.

"That's mine," said Max, eyeing the distinctive Parisian label hand sewn onto the silk.

"I thought you said you never shared your haberdashery."

"I lied. Sue me." Max plucked the tie from Peggy's fingers, carefully folded it, and tucked it in his suit jacket pocket. "I'll tell you this much. The money was marked. I've put one of my best operatives on the case. It's the least I can do to help a good customer."

"What operative? How was the money marked?"

"That's for me to know, and you to find out." With a wink and a wave, Max was gone. A second later he reappeared. "Don't worry about Nicky," Max said softly. "He's a good boy." Another wink, and Max was gone.

Peggy stared at the air in amazement. Her thoughts were interrupted by a ringing phone. It was the medical examiner returning her call. Briefly, she outlined her idea about the gun. The medical examiner was two jumps ahead of her. He promised to let Peggy know the results of the ballistics report.

Peggy spent the rest of the morning waiting on customers and trimming her store window for Thanksgiving. But most of the time, Peggy was thinking about the money. Damn Max, anyway. Why couldn't he ever give a straight answer to a question? About the only thing he said was that the money was marked. How? How much money was there? What denominations? ATMs usually spit out only tens and twenties. Would the money fit into a shoebox? A breadbox? A suitcase? Peggy was convinced that Roger had the money. And that he'd hidden it somewhere. He couldn't have spent all of it. Perhaps three thousand on the computer, stereo, and DVD player. Okay, five thousand, tops. The very idea of a kid spending five thousand dollars on electronic toys made Peggy's blood boil. Knowing it was someone else's hard-earned money obtained under false pretenses made her even madder. Shoveling coal was far too good for Roger Cartwright.

The phone rang.

"What do *you* want?" Peggy barked before she knew who was on the other end of the line. "Oops, sorry. Tom's Tools."

"Peggy," said the medical examiner, "I just got a copy of the ballistics report. The bullet that killed Roger Cartwright was the same caliber as the gun found next to Luigi Alsop."

Peggy's heart sank.

"But it was fired from a different gun."

Chapter 31

"That puts Papa Luigi in the clear, doesn't it?" asked Lavinia, wiping a bit of mayonnaise off her upper lip.

Peggy and Lavinia were sitting in the hardware store, having a late lunch of tuna salad sandwiches Peggy had made that morning.

"The medical examiner seems to think so. But we still don't know who killed Roger Cartwright," replied Peggy. "Could be anyone. I'll bet you anything Maria wasn't the only child Roger bullied. Or the first time he was involved in shady dealings." Peggy giggled.

"What's so funny?"

"Max stopped in this morning. He said Roger will be shoveling coal for all eternity."

Lavinia snorted. "As if Max would know."

"Sometimes I wonder about Max," said Peggy. "He seems to know a lot of things."

"Come on, PJ. What are you saying? That Max has supernatural powers?"

"It's possible."

"Right." Lavinia reached for a handful of chips. "I think you've been spending too much time watching the Sci Fi channel with Nicky. You know what I think about Max? I think he's an eccentric rich man who likes to be mysterious because it makes him the center of attention."

"Lovey, that's not fair."

"Who said anything about fair? I'm trying to be a realist. Max has done wonders for Cobb's Landing, and for that I'm grateful. We all are. If Max wants to run around flapping his arms saying he's an angel with wings, I'll believe it when I see him soaring in the air under his own power. You've always had a vivid imagination, PJ, ever since we were kids. What else did Max say?"

"Max said the money Papa Luigi withdrew from the bank was marked. And he said he had one of his operatives on the case."

Lavinia almost choked on her diet soda. "What is this? A spy novel? Now you're going to tell me that Max is really M from the Ian Fleming books. Who's playing James Bond? Rob Gibson?"

Peggy laughed. "Rob doesn't look like any of the Bonds, and he certainly doesn't have the sexy British accent. He does have the gadgets though. He's got a small battery-operated computer that fits in his hand. It's got a camera and one of those map things. GPS, that's what it's called. Nicky would love it."

"PJ, what did you say about marked money?"

"Max said it, I didn't. Max said the money Papa Luigi got from the bank was marked."

"Marked how?"

"I don't know. Max wouldn't tell me. All he said was 'that's for me to know, and you to find out.' Sometimes I want to strangle Max with his own bow tie." Peggy ate the last bite of her sandwich. "I wish I knew how much money we were talking about."

"One hundred thousand dollars."

Peggy did a double take. "How much?"

"You heard me."

"How do you know the exact amount?"

"I had a long talk with Papa Luigi this morning."

"Papa Luigi had that much money in his bank account?"

Lavinia shook her head. "This is going

to break your heart. Papa Luigi is cash poor and land rich. Only five thousand dollars came from his savings account. And that just about wiped it out."

"Please don't tell me Papa Luigi sold his house to raise the rest of the cash."

"It's almost that bad, PJ. Papa Luigi owned his house and the woods free and clear. He bought the land years ago and paid it off month by month, then built the house with his savings after he retired. He was leaving the house and the woods to Maria to finance her college education. He mortgaged them to raise the cash. He now owes the bank one hundred thousand dollars. That's more money than he can ever repay. Everything he worked for all his life is gone."

"But surely he didn't get that much money in cash?"

"No, he got a certified check."

"Max can stop payment on that check."

Lavinia shook her head. "It's too late. Papa Luigi used that check to buy a bearer bond. One little piece of paper that anyone can cash in."

"Where is it?"

"He doesn't know. He was told to leave it in an envelope in a mailbox at one of those places at the mall where you ship

224

packages. He was then to wait for a wire transfer putting his share of the three point six million dollars into his bank account."

"Did he do it?"

"Yes. He went to the mall late Wednesday afternoon with the envelope. He gave me the key. I checked the box today after I got through at the hospital. The box was empty."

"Oh, Lovey."

"Papa Luigi is so disheartened and feels so foolish. You know what he said? He said he fell for those Nigerian letters because he was afraid Lew wouldn't come home alive from Iraq, and he wanted to provide for Gina and Maria. He wasn't being greedy, PJ; Papa Luigi was doing what he's done all his life. Taking care of his family."

Peggy reached for the open box of Kleenex she kept at the checkout counter. She grabbed a few tissues for herself, then passed the box to Lavinia. They both wiped their eyes and blew their noses.

"This settles it, Lovey. I'm going back inside the Cartwright house. That money has got to be there somewhere. We can't take a chance that anyone will find that bearer bond and cash it."

"We're in this together, PJ. I'm going with you."

The two women spent the rest of the afternoon plotting.

Chapter 32

"Mom, can I go over to Charlie's? Mrs. Cartwright wasn't at school today. We had a substitute, so I don't have any homework."

"Okay, Nicky. But be home by nine. Lavinia and I have to go out for awhile. If I'm not back when you get home, I want you in bed, lights out, no later than nine-thirty. Deal?"

"Deal."

"Don't forget to let Buster in before you go to sleep."

"I won't, Mom."

Peggy and Lavinia got into Peggy's car and headed for the Cartwrights' house.

"How do you know Henry won't be there, PJ?"

"I talked to the medical examiner late this afternoon. Roger's body was being released to the mortuary in Grover's Corners. Henry should be on his way there now to make funeral arrangements."

"This whole thing gives me the creeps, PJ."

"Me, too, Lovey. Tell you what. You wait in the car. If I'm not back in half an hour, call out the cavalry."

Peggy parked on the side street opposite the Cartwrights' where Lavinia had full view of the front of the house. As she got out of the car, Peggy said, "If you see anything suspicious, lay on the horn, then get the hell out of here. I'll find my own way home."

"Be careful."

Peggy nodded, then made her way across the street and around the back of the Cartwright house, having made sure there were no cars parked in the driveway in front. She used the key Carole Ann had given her the day before and let herself in the back door.

The house was completely dark inside.

Peggy crept up the stairs to Roger's room. The padlock was hanging open on the hasp.

Peggy pulled a penlight from her pocket. She'd put in a fresh battery before leaving her house and coated the lens with red nail polish to dim the light.

She began her search. Peggy and Lavinia had spent a good portion of the afternoon trying to think like a seventeen-year-old scam artist. Roger might have been slick, but either he wasn't too bright or else he'd become overconfident of his own invincibility. The jewelry and trinkets he'd bullied from the younger children had been tossed carelessly in his desk drawer, almost in plain sight. Peggy had a hunch the money would be someplace easily accessible.

She first looked under the bed, then between the mattress and box spring. She moved to the desk, quickly opening each drawer and looking behind and underneath for anything taped there. No luck.

That left the closet and all the CD and DVD boxes. Peggy knew she'd never have time to look inside all those plastic boxes. Closet first.

Peggy knelt at the closet entrance, shoved the boots aside, and began examining the closet floor. Having lived in an old house all her life, Peggy knew how meticulously they were constructed. The work was done in an era when attention was paid to small details like the wood grain of a planked floor.

The pattern of one piece of oak on the closet floor was out of line with the others.

Knowing Roger wouldn't have used a nail file to pry it up, Peggy tried pressing down on one end of the wood. The opposite end rose slightly like a teeter-totter.

Peggy pressed again, this time ready to grab the far end. She set the board aside and focused her light on the cavity beneath.

On top was a plain white envelope that had been torn open. Peggy looked inside the envelope. There was the bearer bond. She quickly slid the envelope down the front of her jeans. It felt cool against her skin.

Underneath the envelope was a pile of cash, all twenties. As Peggy began stuffing wads of bills into her jeans, a car horn blared.

Peggy jumped up and left Roger's room. She was halfway down the stairs when the lights went on and there stood Henry, a gun in his right hand pointed straight at Peggy.

"What in the hell are you doing in my house?"

Chapter 33

Peggy knew her goose was cooked.

Henry bounded up the stairs, grabbed Peggy's left arm, twisted it behind her back forcing it up toward her shoulder. Peggy shrieked from the sudden pain.

"Shut up. Any more out of you, and I won't hesitate to use this." Henry shoved the gun at the base of Peggy's spine as he marched her down the stairs. "We're going for a little ride."

Henry holstered his gun and walked Peggy out the front door — making it appear to anyone who might have been looking that he had his arm draped around Peggy in a friendly gesture — never relaxing his hold on her. As he was helping Peggy into the police car, behind the wire grill separating the backseat from the front, Henry applied extra pressure on Peggy's arm. Peggy heard a pop and fell into the backseat, her breath whistling through her clenched teeth. The pain radiating through her shoulder was so intense and excruciating, Peggy fought to remain conscious.

Henry drove into Alsop's woods. The first quarter moon was slipping toward the west, more show than illumination.

Henry stopped the police car. Opening the back door, he pulled Peggy to her feet. Peggy screamed from the pain in her shoulder.

"Scream all you like," said Henry. "There's no one around to hear you." He tied Peggy's wrists in front of her and short-roped her through the woods, holding a flashlight in his free hand.

Peggy tried to get her bearings through the red fog of pain blurring her vision. She had no idea where she was, other than in the woods. She began counting every step she took.

They had gone seventy-eight steps when Henry stopped short. He moved his light around the woods, found what he was looking for, then continued walking. Ten paces later their journey ended inside the cave.

Henry pushed Peggy to the ground and tied her ankles together with the length of rope hanging from her wrists.

Peggy felt like a trussed Thanksgiving turkey.

After sticking the flashlight in the ground, its beam aimed at the cave ceiling to provide ambient light, Henry loomed over Peggy, his hands on his hips. "You just couldn't leave well enough alone, could you? You nosy, interfering busybody. You want to know how my son died? I'll tell you. I killed him."

Peggy willed herself not to make a sound or show any reaction, other than a sympathetic interest, to what Henry was saying. She cocked her head and listened.

"That boy was a bad seed. I couldn't let him ruin my life any longer. All these years I've had to pull up stakes and start over again every time he got in trouble. I finally showed him who was boss, didn't I?"

Henry pulled his gun out of its holster. "By the time anyone finds you, I'll be long gone." Henry took careful aim at Peggy and cocked the trigger.

"Put down that gun immediately. Henry Cartwright, you're under arrest for the murder of your son Roger Cartwright."

Peggy's gaze shifted to Henry's right. Standing there, with a badge in one hand and a gun in the other pointed at Henry, was Missy.

Peggy was never so glad to see someone she so despised.

Henry dropped his gun. Missy slapped handcuffs on Henry and pushed him out of the cave, calling over her shoulder, "Don't move, Peggy, I'll be right back."

Don't move? As if I could, thought Peggy. Despite her pain, Peggy laughed.

Peggy heard other voices approaching the cave entrance. Rob Gibson's was one of them.

Peggy heard Missy say, "You three take Henry to the county jail. I'll stay here and take care of Peggy. Report back to me at the inn after Henry's been booked for murder."

Chapter 34

Missy made her way back inside the cave. She knelt at Peggy's feet and quickly, but gently, untied the rope binding Peggy's ankles and wrists.

"Peggy, do you think you can stand?"

Peggy looked at Missy. "What are you doing here?"

Missy smiled. "It's a long story, Peggy. I'll tell you everything later. But first, let's get you out of here. Are you okay?"

Peggy shook her head. "I don't know what Henry did to me, but my left shoulder hurts like hell. I can't use my arm."

"I'll help you up." Missy moved to Peggy's right side and slid her arm around Peggy's waist, grabbing onto the waistband of Peggy's jeans. "Put your right arm around my shoulders. On the count of three. Okay?" Missy took a deep breath. "One. Two. Three." Missy pulled Peggy to her feet. "The good news is you're standing. The bad news is you're going to have to walk out of the woods. My car is parked not far from Henry's. Do you think you can make it? We'll take it nice and easy."

Missy grabbed the flashlight Henry had left behind. Slowly the two women made their way out of the woods to Missy's car. "Next stop, the hospital," said Missy.

"Lavinia will be worried, I've got to call her," said Peggy. "And Nicky. I need to talk to my son."

"We'll do it from the hospital," said Missy, after helping Peggy into the passenger seat of her sports car. She leaned over and fastened Peggy's seatbelt. "Ready for the ride of your life?" Missy grinned and started her engine.

Missy handled her car and the roads with the finesse of a seasoned pro at Le Mans. "That's my best time yet," she said as she pulled up to a smooth stop in front of the emergency room entrance.

Papa Luigi's doctor was on duty. "You're too late for visiting hours."

Missy took charge. "Peggy needs medical attention. I think she has a dislocated shoulder. But first she needs a phone."

Peggy called her house. No answer. Then she tried the Coopers'. Lavinia answered on the first ring.

"PJ? Where are you? Are you all right?"

"Lovey, I can't talk now. I'm at the hospital. I'll be home soon. Is it okay if Nicky spends the night at your house?"

"Of course it is. I'll wait up for you. You're not going to bed until I've heard about everything that happened tonight."

Back to the emergency room. A nurse showed Peggy into a cubicle. "Take off your clothes and put on this robe so the doctor can examine you. You can keep your shoes on."

"It's only my shoulder that needs examining."

"Hospital rules."

The money. Peggy's jeans were stuffed with money and the envelope containing the bearer bond. Peggy excused herself to use the bathroom before disrobing. She put the money inside the envelope, then stuffed the envelope inside her sneaker. She felt lopsided as she walked, but at least the money was safe.

The doctor popped Peggy's shoulder back into place. The relief from the intense pain was immediate. "It's going to hurt for a couple of days. I want you to wear this sling. Try to get some rest. Don't do anything foolish like pulling clothes off over your head or playing touch football. Here are some pain pills to be taken if needed. Do you have your insurance card with you?"

Missy whipped out a gold card. "This will cover the bill." As an aside to Peggy she whispered, "It's a company card, Max picks up the tab."

"I need to see Papa Luigi," said Peggy.

"Visiting hours are over," said the doctor. "I told you that when you first came in."

Missy flashed her badge. "I think we can make an exception, don't you?"

The doctor grudgingly agreed. "Five minutes. You've got five minutes."

"I'll wait for you outside, Peggy," said Missy.

Peggy went to Papa Luigi's room and tapped on his door. She opened it and poked her head inside. Papa Luigi was sitting up in bed. He smiled wanly at Peggy.

"I don't sleep so good any more," he said.

"Papa Luigi, I think you'll sleep a lot better when you see what I have for you." Peggy bent down and took off her shoe. She removed the envelope and handed it to Papa Luigi.

With shaking fingers he opened the envelope and looked inside. Tears welled in his eyes when he saw the money and the bearer bond.

"There's more money," said Peggy. "I'll get it all for you tonight."

Papa Luigi pushed the envelope back at Peggy. "You keep this in a safe place for me until I'm outta here."

"I promise." Peggy slipped the envelope back inside her jeans. She bent down to hug Papa Luigi with her good arm. "I have more good news for you. The police know who killed Roger Cartwright. Henry confessed tonight and is now in jail." She planted a soft kiss on Papa Luigi's forehead.

Papa Luigi was fast asleep, a gentle smile on his lips, before Peggy was out of the room.

Chapter 35

On the drive back to Cobb's Landing, Peggy turned to Missy. "I can't thank you enough for everything you've done tonight. But there's one thing I need to know right now. Whose side are you on?"

"The side of the angels, Peggy." Missy smiled, keeping her eyes on the road. "Why do you ask?"

"Missy, I'm serious. Who are you working for? What's this badge you keep flashing?"

"Oh, that."

"Yes, that."

"Technically, I work for Max. He pays me. But from time to time he loans me out on special assignments. Does that answer your question?"

"Not really."

"Try this. Tonight I'm working for the U.S. Postal Inspection Service in conjunction with the U.S. Secret Service. That's really as much as I can tell you."

"Missy, I'm trying to help Papa Luigi. A

week ago I saw you outside his house. You were talking to him about final papers and arranging a payoff."

"Mr. Alsop had arranged for a mortgage through the bank. Max asked me to handle the paperwork."

"Do you know what Papa Luigi wanted the money for?"

Missy pulled over to the side of the road, downshifting into neutral. She turned in her bucket seat to look at Peggy. "Peggy, I know all about the Nigerian scam. That's why Max brought me back to Cobb's Landing. He was worried about Mr. Alsop's sudden cash withdrawals from his account. Max is very protective of his investments and the people he cares about. Now I've got a question for you: What do you know that I don't?"

"I know who wrote the letters and where the money is."

"You go, girl!" Missy tapped Peggy lightly on the shoulder with her fist, then clapped her hand over her mouth when she saw Peggy wince. "Peggy, I'm sorry. I forgot about your shoulder."

"I'll survive." Peggy smiled. "Missy, Max told me this morning the money Papa Luigi received was marked. I want to grab the rest of the stash I found before anyone else gets their paws on it. I think that money belongs to Papa Luigi."

"Let's go." Missy shifted into first and eased back onto the road. "Where are we going?"

"Henry Cartwright's house."

Missy let out a whoop. "This is too good to be true. We can nail Henry on fraud *and* murder."

"No, Missy. Roger wrote the letters."

"Roger? Are you sure?"

"Copies of the letters were on Roger's laptop. Tonight I found a cache of money hidden in Roger's closet."

"Where is it now?"

"I've got most of it with me, the rest is still in the closet. Henry caught me inside his house as I was trying to leave."

Missy waved away Peggy's indiscretion with a flip of her hand. "If Henry knows what's good for him, he'll keep his mouth shut. Roger was a minor in the custody of his parents. That puts Henry on the hook. How did you get into Henry's house?"

"I have a key."

"How did you get it?"

"Carole Ann Cartwright gave it to me yesterday. She told me to give it to Henry. I forgot to do it yesterday and tonight it slipped my mind."

"Fair enough." Missy pulled up in front of the Cartwrights' house and parked the car. "Give me the key. I'll unlock the door this time. I've got a warrant. That will keep you out of trouble."

Peggy pulled the key from her jean pocket and put it in Missy's outstretched hand.

For the third time, Peggy entered Roger Cartwright's room. Missy followed behind her. Peggy went straight to the closet and bent down to retrieve the rest of the money from the cache between the joists.

The cache was empty.

Chapter 36

Missy swore under her breath, then muttered aloud. "Let's get the flock out of here."

When they were back in Missy's car, Peggy asked, "Where are we going?"

"The bank."

Missy pulled a sharp U-turn then headed toward Main Street. When she got to the Citizen's Bank, she screeched to a stop. Peggy glanced at the time/temperature on the bank sign and was amazed to discover it was only ten. It felt like two or three in the morning.

Missy made several phone calls. First she called the county police. Henry Cartwright had been brought in, booked, and was behind bars. "That's the good news. Here's the bad news. There is no Robert — or Rob or Bob or Bobby — Gibson on the county force."

"What?"

"Peggy, do you need a pain pill? You look a little gray."

"I'm okay." Peggy paused, then slapped her good hand on the desktop. "No, I'm not okay. I'm not okay at all. I hate being lied to. Whoever that person is — the one calling himself Rob Gibson — he was in my house yesterday. He spent most of the day in my house or Lavinia's. I feel as duped as Papa Luigi."

"Peggy, we'll get back to that later. Max is on his way here right now. He's not going to like this one bit. Max does not tolerate screwups."

Max breezed in looking as fresh as the dew at dawn in a navy suit, fresh white shirt, and his red silk bow tie. "My, my," he chortled, "it's good to see you two working together at last. I hear you have been busy bees tonight."

"Max, we have a problem," said Missy.

"Problem? What problem? You know I don't like that word."

"There's good news and there's bad news," said Missy.

Max glowered.

"The good news: Henry Cartwright is behind bars for the murder of his son Roger. He's already signed a confession. If it goes to court . . ." Missy glanced at Peggy for backup; Peggy nodded, having a good idea what Missy was going to say next. "Peggy and I were witnesses to his verbal confession."

"Very good. What's the bad news?" Max stretched out the word *bad* until it sounded like a goat bleating in a field.

"One of the three police officers who were supposed to transport Henry Cartwright to the county jail is missing. In fact, he may be an imposter."

Max roared. "*What?* How could you let this happen? You're a trained agent." Max was almost purple with rage.

Peggy went to bat for Missy. "Max, Missy saved my life tonight. If it weren't for her, I might be dead or still tied up in that cave with a dislocated shoulder. Missy took me to the hospital. If it's any consolation, I was also taken in by Rob Gibson."

Max's boil subsided to a low simmer.

Peggy reached into the front of her jeans and pulled out the envelope that was now slightly damp with nervous sweat. "There's more good news. I found most of the money that was scammed from Papa Luigi. In that envelope you'll also find a bearer bond he bought with the proceeds of his mortgage. Papa Luigi wants this kept in a safe place until he's out of the hospital."

"Always glad to oblige a good customer," said Max. "Come with me to the vault.

We'll store this in a safe-deposit box immediately. I'll even waive the annual fee."

From the look of relief flooding Missy's face, Peggy knew Missy was back in Max's good graces.

"Max, before you put that envelope away," Missy paused for a breath, "there's something else you should know."

"Missy."

Uh-oh, thought Peggy. Max's blood was on the boil again.

"Peggy didn't get all the money. There was still some left behind. When we went back to retrieve it, it was gone."

"Continue."

In for a penny, in for a pound. Once again, Peggy jumped in to save Missy's hide. "Max. You told me earlier today the money Papa Luigi withdrew was marked. I think the imposter went back to grab what I left behind. Could you look in the envelope to see if what's inside was marked? Then you could circulate a list of the marked bills. It might be a way to trap the imposter."

Max took two twenties from the envelope and left the room. He returned a few minutes later, almost his jovial self. "Good thinking. This *is* part of the marked money. Missy, take care of the details."

Missy headed for her office. Max and Peggy counted the money in the envelope — it came to almost two thousand dollars — then put it in a safe-deposit box along with the bearer bond. Max handed Peggy the key to the box.

"How much did you leave behind?" asked Max.

"Maybe half again as much as I brought here. I think Roger spent some of the money on electronics. He had a pretty fancy stereo and DVD player. And a laptop computer."

"Where is that computer now?"

"Rob Gibson has it."

"Missy!"

Missy came running out of her office. "You bellowed, chief?"

Max grinned. "Missy. I know how much you love playing with your computers. Here's a little job for you. Peggy says that the person calling himself Rob Gibson has Roger Cartwright's laptop."

Missy's eyes gleamed. "I'm on it, chief." She ran back to her office.

"Max, I don't understand."

"Missy is a computer genius. I really don't understand them myself." Max reached over and patted Peggy's good hand. "While Missy works her magic, why don't you go home and get some sleep. You look exhausted. We'll talk again in the morning."

"Max, there's one more thing. Rob Gibson was staying at the inn. At least that's what he told me."

Max grinned. "I'll have Missy drive you home while I make a few calls. If our Mr. Gibson ran off without paying his bill, I'll get him. It's against the law to defraud an innkeeper."

Chapter 37

Lavinia was pacing in Peggy's living room. When she heard a car approach, she ran to Peggy's front door. She watched dumbfounded as Peggy got out of a low-slung black sports car and waved good-bye to the driver. She did a double take when she saw Peggy's arm in a sling. She ran down Peggy's front walk to help her friend.

"Lovey, what are you doing here? Why aren't you asleep?" Peggy whispered.

"Everyone's gone to bed in my house, I didn't want to make any noise. I told you I'd wait up for you."

When they were inside Peggy's house, they resumed normal speech.

"What happened to your arm? Who dropped you off just now? Was that Missy?"

Peggy grinned. "Max offered. But then he remembered he doesn't know how to drive."

"Max doesn't drive?"

Peggy shook her head. "Apparently Max has been chauffeured all his life."

"Poor Max."

"Lovey, would you make me some hot cocoa? With a good splash of brandy in it?"

"Are you taking medication, PJ?"

"No. The doctor gave me some pain pills, but I haven't taken any. I'd rather have the cocoa and brandy."

"Coming right up."

The two women went into Peggy's kitchen. Peggy sat in her favorite chair, not quite knowing where to rest her aching arm.

"PJ, go back in the living room. I'll get some pillows to make you more comfortable." Lavinia ran upstairs to Peggy's bedroom — as familiar to her as her own — and returned with two bed pillows. When Peggy was settled, Lavinia finished making the cocoa.

"Thank you, Lovey." Peggy took a tentative sip to make sure it wasn't too hot. Like Goldilocks' porridge, it was just right. She drained the cup and held it out to Lavinia. "May I have some more?"

When Peggy was sipping her second cup, Lavinia said, "I can't stand it any longer. Tell me what happened!"

"You first, Lovey. You were in the car."

"I must have been daydreaming, PJ, because I never saw Henry drive up the street. I'm sorry I couldn't give you any more warning. When I looked, he'd already parked and was walking up to his front door. I did just what you told me. I started up the car, leaned on the horn, and got the hell out of there. Then I came home and waited for you to call. The waiting drove me crazy. When I didn't hear from you, I called Rob Gibson at the inn."

"You did?"

"I didn't know who else to call. Did I do the right thing?"

"Lovey, you're not going to believe this. That's not the Bobby Gibson we knew. That man who showed up here yesterday at my front door is an imposter. He's probably not even a real police officer."

"You're kidding."

Peggy shook her head. "And that's not all, he may also be a thief."

"Good Lord. I feel like such a fool."

"Don't feel bad, Lovey. You're not the only one who was taken in."

"Okay. Let's pick up where you went to the Cartwright house."

"First, is Nicky okay?"

"PJ, he's fine. He and Charlie spent the evening playing computer games. Then I suggested as long as they were having so much fun, that Nicky spend the night. The boys were asleep before ten. Don't worry, I'll give him breakfast in the morning, and Chuck can drive the boys to school."

"Thanks. I owe you."

"Don't be silly. We do this for each other all the time. Now then. You went into the Cartwrights' house."

"I found where Roger had hidden the money."

Lavinia let out a deep sigh of relief. "Papa Luigi will be so pleased."

"He already knows, Lovey. There's better news than that. I also found the bearer bond."

Lavinia grinned from ear to ear. "Can I see it?"

"It's locked away in a safe-deposit box at the bank." Peggy fished down the neck of her sweater and pulled out a silver chain. Hanging from the chain was the key to the safe deposit box. "Anyone — aside from Papa Luigi, of course — who tries to get this key is going to have to decapitate me."

Lavinia laughed. "So what does it look like?"

"What?"

"A bearer bond. I've never seen one."

"It's a regular-sized piece of paper, the fancy kind with engraving and all that stuff. Just think. That one piece of paper is worth one hundred thousand dollars."

"What did you do when you found it?"

"I stuffed the envelope down the front of my jeans."

Lavinia clapped her hands. "I love it. Where did you find it?"

"Lovey, you're really going to love this part. It was underneath a floorboard in Roger's closet. I discovered his hidey-hole because the wood grain didn't match. He must have been in a hurry and put the board back the wrong way around."

"Nancy Drew would be proud of you, PJ."

"The money was there, too. What was left of it. Max and I counted about two thousand dollars. I was just beginning to stuff wads of twenties into my jeans when I heard the car horn."

"What did you do?"

"I started to get the hell out of there. I left the rest of the money where I found it and beat feet for the stairs."

"What happened then?"

"I was halfway down the stairs when the lights went on, and there was Henry. He had his gun drawn, pointed right at me." Peggy giggled. "I almost wet my pants then and there, but I didn't want to ruin the bond." Peggy held out her empty cocoa cup.

"PJ, I think you've had enough brandy for one night. You're starting to get punchy. Are you sure you didn't take any pain pills?"

"Positive."

"Did the doctor give you a shot?"

Peggy shook her head.

"Okay. One more cup of cocoa on the way."

Lavinia brought the cocoa and the brandy bottle. "You and Henry were on the stairs."

"That's when Henry twisted my arm."

"He what?"

"He grabbed my left arm and pulled it behind my back, shoving it almost up to my shoulder blade."

"Ouch."

"You're damned right, ouch. When we got out to the police car, that bastard gave it an extra push. That's when I heard a popping sound. I thought I was going to pass out from the pain. He drove to Alsop's woods and parked the cruiser. Then he tied my wrists together in front of me and led me to the cave. It wasn't the same way we went on Saturday along the river. Henry knew a shortcut from the opposite direction."

"You spent all that time with a dislocated shoulder?" Lavinia opened the brandy bottle and added a splash to Peggy's cocoa. "You've earned this. Drink up."

"When we were inside the cave, Henry tied my ankles. That's when he confessed that he killed Roger."

"Holy crap. Henry did it? He killed his son?"

Peggy nodded before reaching for her cocoa cup. "He said Roger was a bad seed who was ruining Henry's life. I think he was planning on killing me, too, but Missy saved the day."

Lavinia gulped. "Missy?"

"Keep this under your hat, Lovey. I'm not sure how much Missy would want me to say. Max brought Missy back to Cobb's Landing because he thought Papa Luigi was being scammed."

"Missy?"

"Yes, Lovey, Missy. Can you believe it? She's got some connection with the Feds. Anyway, Missy pulled her own gun on Henry, put him under arrest, and slapped handcuffs on him."

"Missy?"

Peggy laughed. "Lovey, will you stop saying that? I think we've misjudged Missy.

There's a lot more to her than we first thought."

Lavinia sat shaking her head. "I can't get over this. Missy?" Lavinia caught the look on Peggy's face. "Okay, okay. I'll stop saying it."

"Missy marched Henry out of the cave. That's when I heard other voices, including Rob Gibson's. Or whoever he is. Apparently there were three men. Missy told them to take Henry to the county police station and report back to her later. Then she untied me and took me to the hospital. That's when I called you."

"When I phoned Rob — let's keep calling him Rob for now, okay? It's easier. Anyway, when I phoned him at the inn, he sounded very concerned and said he'd start looking for you right away."

"I told you he had a map device on that computer thing of his. When I showed him the cave yesterday, he made a mark on his map. He could have found the cave again blindfolded." Peggy sipped her cocoa.

"After the hospital, Missy and I went back to the Cartwrights' to retrieve the last of the money in Roger's hidey-hole. But when we got there, it was empty."

"How could that be, PJ?"

"Beats me. Roger is dead, Henry was on

the way to jail, Carole Ann split for Lord knows where. The only other person I know of who was in that room recently was Rob."

"Sounds like the name suits him," said Lavinia with a disdainful sniff.

Peggy smiled. "Missy and I went directly to the bank. When she called the county police to make sure Henry had been booked and was behind bars, that's when she found out there was no one working there named Rob Gibson. Boy, do I feel dumb. When he showed up on my door-step yesterday he was in uniform. He said he was from the county. I believed him. I never asked to see his identification."

"Don't be so hard on yourself, PJ. If he faked the uniform, he probably had a fake ID as well."

"But how did he know so much about us? We haven't talked about Bobby Gibson in years. Not until Saturday night when we were sitting in your kitchen. It's really creepy that he would show up in the flesh the very next morning."

"You're the one who believes in woo-woo, PJ. Let's get some sleep. I'll go up and get you a blanket. You'll probably be more comfortable tonight if you sleep sit-ting up." Lavinia tucked the blanket around her friend and turned off the lights. "I'll come over tomorrow morning and help you get dressed."

Chapter 38

Nicky was surprised to find his mother sleeping sitting up in the living room when he came home Tuesday morning to change clothes for school.

"Mom! Are you sick?"

Peggy opened her eyes. "Nicky. What time is it?"

"It's seven-thirty, Mom. I've got to get dressed for school. I already had breakfast with Charlie."

"That's good. What did you have?"

"Juice, cereal, toast. You know. Breakfast stuff."

Peggy began to stretch, then yelped and clutched her left arm. "I shouldn't have done that."

"What happened to your arm?"

"Nicky, it's nothing. I pulled a muscle and went to the hospital to have it checked out. The doctor wants me to wear a sling for a couple of days."

"That's cool, Mom. I wish I had one. Then I wouldn't have to do any homework again. Ever."

"In your dreams, Nicky." Peggy smiled at her son. "Go get dressed for school. I'll make your lunch."

"That's okay. Charlie's mom made one for me, and his dad is going to take us to school."

Nicky ran up the stairs to his bedroom.

Lavinia came in through the kitchen. "How are you feeling?"

"Okay, I guess. A little stiff and my arm aches this morning."

"I'm not surprised. I brought you a pot of coffee."

"You're a lifesaver, Lovey."

"Don't mention it. I'll be back after the boys have left for school."

Nicky came bounding down the stairs. "I did everything, Mom. Hair, teeth, hands, and face. How do I look?"

"You look terrific. Give me a kiss before you go."

"Mom, you haven't brushed your teeth yet. You've got bat breath."

Peggy smiled at their old private joke. "Fair enough, Nicky. But I get two kisses tonight."

"Okay, Mom." Nicky hugged his mother. "See you!"

Peggy dragged herself off the couch. All

she wanted to do was curl up and sleep the day away. She couldn't remember the last time she'd done that. She pulled the blanket and pillows up the stairs behind her. Having full use of only one arm was a very strange sensation. Peggy managed to brush her teeth and hair and change into clean underwear and jeans by herself. To hell with it, she'd wear the same pullover sweater two days in a row.

Peggy was down in the kitchen when Lavinia came through the back door.

"Want me to help you with that sweater? It would be easier if you wore something that buttoned down the front rather than being pulled over your head."

The front doorbell rang. "You sit down, PJ, I'll see who's at the door."

Lavinia came back into the kitchen. "PJ, it's Missy."

"Let her in, Lovey."

Lavinia was followed by Missy. "Peggy, I hope I'm not here too early. First, I wanted to find out how you were feeling."

"I've had better days," Peggy said with a smile. "Missy, you look like something the cat dragged in. Did you get any sleep last night?"

"PJ," said Lavinia, "I'll be next door if you need anything."

"Lovey, don't be a silly goose." Peggy turned to Missy. "Missy, you remember my friend and neighbor Lavinia Cooper? Lovey, I'm sure you remember Missy. Enough of the social introductions. Missy, help yourself to a cup of coffee. You look like you really need one."

The three women sat at Peggy's kitchen table drinking coffee. Finally Peggy broke the silence. "Missy, I've known Lovey since we were kids. She's my best friend. Anything you want to say to me, you can say in front of her."

Missy smiled. "I've got good news and bad news."

Peggy laughed. "Where have I heard that before? Let's start with the bad news."

"Henry Cartwright committed suicide last night in his jail cell."

Peggy and Lavinia stared at Missy. "You can't be serious. How did it happen?"

"He hung himself."

"Oh." Peggy exhaled slowly. "After what he did to his son, I shouldn't feel sorry for Henry, but I do. That whole family was a tragedy."

Lavinia nodded in agreement.

"I hate to ask about the good news," said Peggy.

"The man passing himself off as Robert

Gibson is in custody at the county jail. That's the good news. The bad news is I need you to come and identify him in a lineup. Are you up to it?"

"I will be after another cup of coffee," said Peggy.

Lavinia got up and put the coffee pot on the table.

"Lavinia saw him, too, Missy. I want her to come with me."

"I'll do it," said Lavinia.

"Did he have any distinguishing marks that you remember?" asked Missy.

"Yes," said Lavinia. "He had a mole next to his left ear. Right here." Lavinia pointed to the spot next to her own ear.

"That's good," said Missy.

"How did he get caught?" asked Peggy.

"Stupidity," said Missy. "You're going to love this. While I was driving you home last night, he tried to pay his hotel bill at the inn with the marked money. You might say Max caught him red-handed."

Peggy shook her head in disbelief. "Missy, what I don't get is why he came to Cobb's Landing in the first place? How did he know so much about us?"

"You'll know more about this than I do," said Missy. "You met the real Robert Gibson when?"

"The summer Peggy and I were twelve," said Lavinia. "Bobby Gibson spent that summer across the street with his grandparents."

"Did you ever see or hear from him again?"

"Not until Sunday morning," said Peggy. "Lovey and I hadn't talked about him in years. His name just happened to come up in conversation Saturday evening and Sunday morning there he was. It was a little unsettling."

"As close as I can figure out, the story goes something like this," said Missy. "At one point the real Bobby and the fake Rob were roommates. The real Bobby died in a car accident a year ago. I ran the fake Rob's prints early this morning. He's got a sheet as long as your arm. One of his specialties is impersonation. With all the tourists who have been here the past few months, the fake Rob probably blended in with the crowd. Peggy, I'm guessing he overheard one of your phone conversations at the hardware store and decided to play policeman. It's not the first time he's impersonated a cop. One quick score and he's gone. He wouldn't have stayed here long. Max will see to it he's put away for a long time."

"Chuck smelled something fishy about him on Sunday."

"What was that, Lovey?"

"No one named Rob Gibson ever played outfield for the Boston Red Sox."

Missy laughed. "See what I mean? Stupidity. The dumb ones always get caught." She turned to Peggy. "Next time be more careful about the people you let in your front door." Missy took her coffee cup over to the kitchen sink. "Thanks for the coffee. See you two at the bank in an hour?"

Max was all smiles when Peggy and Lavinia walked into the bank. "Just the two I wanted to see. I know it's short notice, but I'm having a small dinner party at the inn tonight, and I would be honored if you would attend. Peggy, I insist that you bring Nicky. Lavinia, I'm counting on seeing Chuck and Charlie. Shall we say six o'clock? I promise you, it'll be an evening you won't want to miss."

"Max," said Peggy. "Are you being mysterious again?"

Max grinned. "That's for me to know, and for you to find out."

Chapter 39

The lineup at the county police station was over in less than five minutes. Peggy and Lavinia immediately spotted the fake Rob and identified him.

"Thank you for doing this," said Missy. "Max never forgets a favor. He owes you both."

"PJ, let's get a move on. I've got to get to the hospital if I'm going to get home in time to change for dinner."

"Lavinia, I'll drive Peggy. I'm heading right back to Cobb's Landing; it would be out of your way."

"You're sure?"

"Positive."

"PJ, go easy on your shoulder. I'll be over to help you dress for dinner." Lavinia got in her car and headed for the hospital.

"Peggy, I'm glad we had time for a chat," said Missy, on the way back to Cobb's Landing. "I'm leaving tonight after the dinner party for a new assignment. Max has given me a promotion. I wanted to thank you for helping defuse Max last night. You really didn't have to do that."

"After what you did for me? It was the least I could do."

"I'm sorry we didn't get to be friends the last time I was here."

"Me, too," said Peggy. "I'm sorry you're leaving Cobb's Landing."

"Who knows? I may be back. You know Max." Missy smiled. "This is probably none of my business, but I'm going to say it anyway."

"What?"

"It's about Ian."

"Oh."

"Hear me out. I know you probably think I came back to make trouble for you two, but nothing could be further from the truth. I really love my older brother, and I want him to be happy."

Peggy was so surprised she almost swallowed her tongue. "Your older brother?"

"You didn't know?"

"How would I know that?" asked Peggy. "No one ever said anything."

"You mean Max never told you?" Missy chuckled. "That Max. He's such a devil."

"Ian is your brother?"

"Peggy, you didn't think . . ."

"I don't know what I thought."

"Ian and I have always been very close. He really cares for you, Peggy. Give him a chance. For what it's worth, you have my blessing."

"It means a lot, Missy. Thank you."

"Where do you want me to drop you? Home or the hardware store?"

"Hardware store, thanks. Missy, tell me something," said Peggy. "What's going on with this dinner party tonight? I'm always glad for a night when I don't have to cook, but why is Max being so mysterious?"

Missy shrugged and smiled. "Max does love his little secrets. I'll see you tonight at the inn."

Peggy spent her time at the hardware store drawing on her sketchpad. When she was finally satisfied, she put the sketch in a frame — not an easy task with her bum shoulder — wrapped it in tissue and put it in her tote to take home.

What to wear to dinner? Was it too early for velvet? What went with a sling? A sarong. Peggy giggled. Definitely not the season for a sarong. She pawed through her closet. Not that she had that much to choose from. Dress-up occasions were few and far between in Peggy's life. Her black velvet skirt and black silk blouse would have to do. Forget pumps, I'll never get on a pair of pantyhose with one good arm. Pantyhose were a two-handed task. Forget the skirt. Peggy got out her good black pants, black boots, and her black velvet jacket. Then she went to Nicky's room and laid out his clothes on his bed.

"Hi, Mom, I'm home! Where are you?"

"I'm upstairs. Get up here. We're going out to dinner at the inn tonight."

"We are? I was going to play with Charlie."

"Don't you have homework?"

"Nah. We had a substitute again today. You know what I heard, Mom? Mrs. Cartwright went away and isn't coming back. Does that mean I'm going to have another new teacher?"

"Probably, sweetie. Let's hope it's someone you really like." Peggy looked at the clock. "You can go and play with Charlie, but you must be home no later than five. You have to take a bath and get dressed for dinner. I got out your gray pants and your navy blazer."

Nicky made a face.

"Nicky, I'll tell you a secret."

"What's that, Mom?"

"I think maybe Maria's going to be there, too."

"Awesome! I'll be home before five."

Nicky kept his word and was home before five. He spent more time primping than Peggy. By six they were walking into the inn. Peggy's hunch proved correct. Gina and Maria were already there, talking to Max who looked elegant in a black tuxedo, accented with his usual red silk bow tie.

The rest of the group included Lavinia, Chuck, and Charlie.

A table for twelve was set up in the candlelit dining room. A cheerful fire burned in the stone fireplace, its flames reflected in the windows overlooking the Rock River. In the corner a string quartet played softly.

Peggy quickly counted on the fingers of her good hand. There were only eight dinner guests. Who else was Max expecting?

Ian and Missy arrived a few minutes after six. That made ten. There were still two empty places.

Max opened a bottle of champagne for the adults and sparking cider for the children. As Max was pouring the champagne, Peggy heard the sound of an approaching helicopter. Max handed the champagne bottle to Ian and quickly left the room.

Max returned a few minutes later and stood at the entrance to the dining room. "Ladies and gentlemen, my dear friends," Max intoned, "may I present our guests of honor for the evening?"

Max stepped aside with a flourish.

There stood Papa Luigi holding onto the arm of a National Guard officer in full-dress uniform.

"Lew!"

"Daddy!"

Peggy felt tears begin to well. A voice behind her said, "take this" and handed her a spotless white handkerchief. Peggy looked up and smiled at Ian. Missy silently applauded.

Max's dinner party was a rousing success. Gina and Maria scarcely ate a bite, they were too overwhelmed by Lew's unexpected — and very welcome — return.

Peggy was seated between Ian and Missy. "All right, you two, tell me. How did Max pull this one off? Gina said Lew wasn't due home for two more months."

Ian smiled. "Max has friends in very high places who owe him big favors."

Peggy knew better than to press the matter. She handed the tissue-wrapped package to Missy.

"What's this?"

"Something I thought you might enjoy as a souvenir of this trip to Cobb's Landing."

Missy tore off the tissue. The sketch showed a Halloween pumpkin bobbing on the Rock River, carved with Missy's face. Attached to the pumpkin was a blue ribbon.

Missy howled with laughter and hugged Peggy. "By the way," Missy whispered, "I'm the one who sent you one of Max's bow ties for your store window. Don't ever tell him." Peggy mimed locking her lips and throwing away the key.

After the dessert — Baked Alaska on fudge brownies — was served, Max made an announcement.

"This year we're going to have an authentic First Thanksgiving feast on the town square. The tourists will eat it up. Tick tock, tick tock, people. We've got three weeks to pull it together."

Chapter 40

Nicky and Charlie were fast asleep in their own beds, Chuck was dozing over the late news on television, Peggy and Lavinia were having a final cup of coffee in Lavinia's kitchen.

"I've got to hand it to Max," said Lavinia. "He really pulled off the surprise of the year. Every time I think of the expression on Gina's face when she saw Lew standing next to Papa Luigi, it makes me want to cry."

"I know what you mean," said Peggy. "Everything worked out all right for the Alsops. I'm so relieved. I'm also glad to be rid of the safe-deposit box key. I gave it to Papa Luigi after dinner. He's paying off the mortgage tomorrow morning. Life is back to normal."

"Except for one thing. We need a new police chief in Cobb's Landing."

"Oh, Lovey, don't even mention it. It's the last thing I want to think about tonight."

"I think you'd better read this." Lavinia handed Peggy an opened envelope. "It arrived in today's mail."

Peggy quickly scanned the enclosed letter. "It's from Stu McIntyre. He wants to come home to Cobb's Landing, and he wants his job back? I'm speechless."

"What do you think, PJ?"

"Lovey, I think we've found ourselves a new police chief."

"Better the devil we know —" said Lavinia.

"Oh, look!" said Peggy. "It's beginning to snow."

Peggy and Lavinia ran outside and stood with upraised faces, tongues outstretched, trying to catch the fat, white flakes swirling lazily around them. It was the same thing they'd done every year at the first snowfall since they were children.

Winter had come to Cobb's Landing.

The employees of Thorndike Press hope you have enjoyed this Large Print book. All our Thorndike and Wheeler Large Print titles are designed for easy reading, and all our books are made to last. Other Thorndike Press Large Print books are available at your library, through selected bookstores, or directly from us.

For information about titles, please call:

(800) 223-1244

or visit our Web site at:

www.gale.com/thorndike
www.gale.com/wheeler

To share your comments, please write:

Publisher
Thorndike Press
295 Kennedy Memorial Drive
Waterville, ME   04901